W9-ADX-943

A PILE OF STONES

A Pile of Stones

SHORT STORIES

BY HUGH NISSENSON

Charles Scribner's Sons
New York

A-3.65[C]

PRINTED IN THE UNITED STATES OF AMERICA
LIBRARY OF CONGRESS CATALOG CARD NUMBER 65-12690

For

my Mother and Father

The stories in this book were first published in the following magazines: "The Groom on Zlota Street" and "The Law" in *Commentary;* "The Blessing" and "The Well" in *Harper's Magazine;* "A Pile of Stones" in *Esquire;* and "The American" in *American Judaism.* "The Prisoner" is included in the 1964 edition of *Stanford Short Stories,* edited by Wallace Stegner and Richard Scowcroft. The author would like to thank the editors of these publications for their appreciation and encouragement.

"Let me go, for the day breaketh."

—GENESIS

Contents

THEN: POLAND

The Groom on Zlota Street

IN THE first decade of the century, when he was twelve years old, my father, his parents, and his cousin Yecheil all lived in a little shop on Mila Street in Warsaw where my grandfather made carriage whips. Just across the way was the entrance to a Russian military barracks, a huge gray stone building with an iron gate that was always guarded by two armed sentries whose hobnailed boots rang out on the cobblestones as they paced up and down at their posts. Every morning, just after dawn, the boy peered breathlessly through the cellar window in order to be able to give Yecheil the signal that the soldiers were at the opposite end of the street and it was safe for him to leave the shop and peddle the whips all over the city.

"Now, David?"

"Not yet," said the boy and Yecheil yawned, slipped the pack off his back, and rubbed his narrow shoulders where the straps had already begun to cut into them.

"Well?"

"They're almost at the gate."

"No rush. No rush. Just tell me when," said Yecheil, fingering his scraggly beard.

"Did they hurt you very much yesterday?"

"No, no."

"I'll never understand it."

"What?"

"If the soldiers keep pulling your beard, why don't you shave it off?"

There was no answer. For as long as the boy had known him, Yecheil had made no concession to modernity. He dressed in a gabardine and skullcap, his ritual locks curled behind his ears, and a razor had never touched his beard. But with a beard like that the boy couldn't see the difference. It looked as if Yecheil had shaved anyway, or worse—begun without finishing the job. For some reason he was unable to grow any hair on his cheeks. It grew in black tufts on his lower jaws, and beneath his chin, accentuating his sharp cheekbones, and long naked face.

"I have to go toward the Prospect this morning. Tell me—the one on the right, what does he look like?"

"I think it's the same one as yesterday," said the boy.

"Are you sure?"

"Yes," said David, but it was a lie. He was never able to tell one of the soldiers from the other. From that distance, and looking up as he did from just above the level of the street, their features were always indistinct and somehow generalized into bristling black mustaches and shaven chins. They wore long black coats with flaring skirts belted at the waist, and their lambskin caps made them seem even taller than they were, not men at all, as far as the boy was concerned, but giants left over from that time recorded in the Bible when giants roamed the face of the earth and loved the daughters of men.

"The same one," said Yecheil. "Is that so? He's not too bad. A Ukrainian by his accent. What's the matter?"

"He's looking this way."

"Never mind. Never mind."

"He's stopped," said David. "No, he's started again. He's almost passed the butcher's. Why does he keep looking over here?"

"The Ukrainian, eh?" Yecheil muttered.

"How can I be sure?"

"No matter, it can't be helped," said Yecheil, slipping on his pack. The tips of the long whips grazed the ceiling. "Come, smile, why don't you? It makes no difference. God be praised. God provides. There's always the groom on Zlota Street."

"The who?"

"Did you say your prayers this morning? We must thank Him for that."

"For what?"

But muttering under his breath, Yecheil was already halfway up the creaking stairs. The boy pressed his cheek against the cold glass and listened to the voices coming faintly from above; his father, giving last-minute instructions, perhaps, or just saying good-by; his mother, calling out from the kitchen, "ooo" —the last, attenuated syllable of some inaudible phrase. Then, to the clatter of the cracked tin bell, the front door was opened and closed, and David peered up and to the right to catch a glimpse of Yecheil hesitating in the doorway of the shop. With his hands thrust under his armpits, he stamped his feet up and down. The icy wind off the river, blowing in gusts from the east, caught at his scraggly beard. "What's he waiting for? Go on. Go now," thought the boy. It was either now or never. Across the narrow street the sentry was coming toward him. The thin bayonet fixed to the end of his rifle glinted in the sun. "Oh now," David prayed, "please now," and, as if in answer, Yecheil turned toward the right and began to walk, a little sideways, keeping as close as he could to the front of the shops. He passed the cobbler's, and Jacobson the hatter's, whose red-lettered sign hung on one hinge and swung in the wind. The butcher's was next. Then he was lost to sight, and all that the boy could see of him was his shadow gliding obliquely across the ground. Then that too was gone. He had passed the tailor shop. David raised his eyes to the sentry. The man had stopped.

"But it might be all right. It might be the Ukrainian after all," he thought. "I must go up." With one last glance, aware that he had shouted aloud, he backed away from the window and stumbled up the stairs into the kitchen. Facing the tailor shop, with his legs spread, the sentry had taken the rifle from his shoulder and was holding it in his hands.

"But it's nothing," said his father.

"Papa, let me go."

"It's nothing, I tell you; David, be still."

"Let go of my arm."

"There's nothing you can do."

"What are they doing to him?"

"Nothing."

"Then let me see."

"Be still."

"Mama!" the boy cried out. "Mama, make Papa let me go."

His mother was standing by the wooden tub, her arms wet to the elbows from washing the breakfast dishes.

"Listen to your father. Be quiet. Hush," she said, drying her hands on her apron, and going to the curtained window to peer out.

"Are they hurting him? Mama? What's happened?"

Her lips twitched, and her face had gone pale, bringing out the dark, wrinkled circles under her eyes.

"They've finished with him," she said. "Ah, there, you see? There he goes. He's gotten away. He's running toward the Prospect."

"Let me see."

"Abba, it's all right," she said. "They've let him go. Let him go."

"Yes, let go," said the boy, wrenching himself free and losing his balance.

"Be careful. The tub!" his mother cried.

"Are you all right?" asked his father. "David?"

"I banged my funny bone."

"Stand up."

"Did they hurt him?"

"Sipra," said his father, "come away from the window. Let me see the arm, David. Stand up. Stand by me."

They went to work in the other room where long strips of rawhide hung from wooden dowels on the walls. The boy had been taught to curry the strips with a sharp, curved knife, scraping them as clean as he could in preparation for his father who attached them as lashes to the ends of a bundle of birch rods. There was no stove in the room. In the morning, they moved their bench to be warmed by the sunlight that streamed through the single oval window over the door. In the afternoon, it grew so cold that they could see their own breath. The boy suffered from chilblain. His fingers became red and puffy. It was awkward and painful to handle the knife and he often cut himself. His father worked opposite him, holding the rod between his knees and one end of the lash taut between his strong white teeth. He was a handsome man with wide dark eyes and a curly black beard with streaks of auburn in it—the color of David's hair. "My beard will be like that, a little redder, maybe, but thick too," the boy thought to himself with a twinge of shame for feeling grateful that he didn't take after Yecheil, his mother's side of the family.

"Papa?"

"Unhh?"

"Just for a minute. Take it out of your mouth."

"How's the elbow?"

"Better, thank you. Papa, I've been thinking. Maybe Yecheil ought to speak to the rabbi."

"What for?"

"I don't know. If he explained, maybe the rabbi would give him permission to shave off his beard."

"Are you finished with that strip?"

"Papa?"

"What is it now?"

"Nothing. I'm finished," said the boy. He should have known better than to even mention it. It was forbidden, and that's all there was to it. How could a Jew shave off his beard? Still—no, the boy decided, and in any case the less said about Yecheil in his father's presence the better. He sensed that his father suffered from the shame of giving in to his wife's fears and, to calm her, swearing on his life never to accompany her nephew to the end of the street in the morning no matter what the soldiers did to him. She was convinced that they would murder her husband as he returned to the shop alone.

At five o'clock they heard the bells of St. Stephan's, the church on the next street, calling the Christians of the neighborhood to Mass. The room was getting dark. It was time to quit. Soon the sun would set and most of the Jewish men on the block would gather in the wooden synagogue on the corner to say their evening prayers. There were fifteen or twenty of them. The Russian sentries who had begun their night watch an hour before rarely dared to molest them in a group.

"Don't look so worried," his father said as he left for the synagogue. "Yecheil will be there. We'll bring him safely home."

In the kitchen, a pan of fat was cooking on the stove.

"What's for dinner?" David asked his mother.

"Your prayers first," she said, putting his skullcap on the back of his head.

"What is it? Tell me. Not potato pancakes again! That's the third time this week. Is there any jam?"

But with her head covered by a cotton scarf, and

her eyes closed, his mother was already absorbed in prayers of her own. David bowed his head, rocked back and forth on his heels and the balls of his feet, listening to the sputtering fat. The heat of the stove swelled his reddened fingers and made them ache even worse than before. He rubbed them together.

"Mama?"

"Finished so soon?"

He hadn't even been able to begin. There were tears in the corners of her eyes. Her lips twitched. For the first time, the boy realized that it had become habitual. Aware all at once of his astonished, stricken glance, she coughed nervously, concealing her mouth behind her hand.

"Oh, Mama."

She blamed herself. He was sure of it. It had never been so clear to him. Rather than blame God, she took the whole thing on herself—not only her husband's shame, but Yecheil's suffering as well. And in a way she was right. It had all begun with an act of kindness on her part, a promise that she had made to her dying sister to provide a home for her unmarried son. Originally from Vilna, left all alone after he had lost his mother in a spotted-fever epidemic some six months before, Yecheil had only come to Warsaw at his aunt's invitation. The trouble was that the shop on Mila Street could barely support three as it was.

Peddling the whips, submitting to the soldiers, was absolutely the only thing that could be found for Yecheil to do.

"Mama, listen to me."

"Wash your hands and come and sit down."

"Listen for a minute. You're not to blame."

"There's a fresh piece of soap in the cupboard."

"You did your best. How can you think it's your fault?"

"No, no. To the left. That's it. Behind the cups."

"Are you listening?"

"What is it?"

"Nobody's to blame because there's nothing else we can do."

"Can you reach it?"

"No."

"Stand on the chair."

"Anyway, if Yecheil doesn't mind so much, why should you? Did he ever tell you about the groom on Zlota Street?"

"Be careful."

"Ask him about that, why don't you?" said David. "We have to be thankful for what we can."

But later, as usual, she ate her supper in silence. No one said anything until Yecheil took a huge bite from the last brown cake on the plate, wiped his greasy fingers on his beard, and turned to her husband.

"There's a new stable on Iron Street, did I tell you? I was there for over an hour this morning, talking to the groom. He comes from Vilna too."

"Is that so? Did he buy anything?"

"He will. He will, absolutely, I'm sure of it. He told me to come back and see him sometime next week."

"Who bought something today?"

"Tomorrow," said Yecheil, blowing into his steaming glass of tea. "Tomorrow will be a good day."

"Really?" asked David. "How many whips will he buy?"

"Who?"

"Why, the groom on Zlota Street. Isn't that where you're going?"

"Who told you about him?"

"You did. Don't you remember? This morning."

"Did I?" said Yecheil. "Ah, if I want, the groom on Zlota Street would buy them all."

"What did I tell you? Mama, did you hear?" asked the boy.

He was unable to sleep. For half the night, tossing and turning on the narrow bed he shared with Yecheil in the closet next to the workroom, he lay awake while the mice scampered across the floor and gnawed the scraps of leather left under the bench. Tomorrow was Friday, Sabbath eve, when Yecheil usually came home early to go to the *mikveh,* the bathhouse just off Marshalkovska Street, for his ritual bath. "Dear God," the boy prayed, "my Father in Heaven, if it's really true, then let him go to Zlota Street first, and sell all of his whips." He blessed the groom, and the stable, and the man's wife, if he was married, and all of their children. "It's not for me that I ask, I swear it. If the groom buys all the whips, that'll mean five or six rubles at least, maybe more. Think what that will mean to Mama. It will be a sign to her, a miracle to celebrate the Sabbath." He shut his eyes and tried to imagine his mother's joy at being able to prepare and bless a full Sabbath meal for the family, a real dinner with fish and wine, chopped herring for an appetizer, garlic and chicken fat spread on thin slices of white bread, potato *kugel,* and a roast chicken. "Why, there'll even be enough money left over for Mama to buy flour and bake a cake. A nut cake with almonds and raisins. . . . Lord, God of my Fathers, do I have to tell You? You know how much it would mean to her—to all of them. . . . Thou art just. I ask You—no matter what happens, do we ever question that? Be Thou merciful too. . . ."

He had involuntarily spoken aloud. Yecheil stirred, snorted once through his nose, and again lay still, with his face to the wall. The mice squeaked. It was bitterly cold. The boy repeated the prayer over and over. Outside, it had begun to rain, and the hollow drumming on the kitchen window filled the whole house.

"Awake? Good morning," said his father, standing at the door. A diffused, dirty light flooded the room. David sat up and rubbed his eyes. He was alone in bed.

"What happened? Is he gone?"

"You overslept."

"When did Yecheil go?"

"Almost an hour ago. . . . No, no, it's all right. You needn't look like that. Nothing happened. It's snowing. The soldiers have built a fire by the gate. Would you believe it? They were too busy warming themselves. They didn't even look at him as he went by."

The boy jumped out of bed and ran to the kitchen window. It was true. His heart leapt. A bonfire blazed in front of the gate, hissing and smoking in the falling snow. The two sentries, with their caps pulled down over their ears, had leaned their rifles against the wall, and were warming their hands.

"They really didn't touch him?"

"Not so much as a glance."

Again David parted the curtain and gazed out of the window. He could hardly believe it. For the first time in over a week the soldiers hadn't molested Yecheil, and on today of all days. He was afraid to think. Was it a good omen, or what?

"Did Yecheil say when he'd be back?"

"It's Friday. Early, I suppose," said his father, and the boy scrutinized his face. He was nibbling on his mustache. Perhaps Yecheil had said nothing to his parents, intending to surprise them, and then again —the boy shook his head. All through the morning he could hardly keep his mind on his work. Again and again, he pictured the Sabbath table, lit by candles, with its loaf of bread covered by a linen napkin, ready to be blessed. He saw his father, dressed in a clean kaftan, with his beard combed, raise his wine glass, and his mother's smiling face. The roast chicken, simmering in the pan, rose before his eyes. His mouth watered, and then all at once, seized by fear, he raised his eyes to the worm-eaten beams of the ceiling over his head.

"How could I? God forgive me," he prayed. In his weakness, he knew that he had jeopardized everything, revealing to God that he had prayed the whole night through not for the relief of his parents, or the sanctification of the Sabbath, but for the gratification of his own desire. The image of the chicken tormented him. He felt the crisp skin melt on his tongue, the bones crunch between his teeth. Try as he would, it was impossible to think of anything else. By noon, he felt exhausted by the effort, and the lack of sleep, and his heart shrank as he heard his mother in the kitchen, scrubbing the floor, already at work on her hands and knees to prepare the house for the Day of Rest. He went in to help her.

"Shall I make a fire?"

"Take off your dirty shoes and move the table out of the way."

Yes. It seemed to him appropriate to walk on his bare feet, as though on holy ground. He moved the table, and piled all the chairs in the corner and went down on his hands and knees himself to scrub the soapy floor. "Strength. Give me strength," he prayed, resisting the temptation to ask his mother what they were going to eat. He fed the fire, and took down the cups to dust the cupboard and slowly but surely, as always just before the Sabbath, the immaculate kitchen calmed his nerves. He could see his face reflected from the pots and pans, the spoons in the drawer. The wooden floor shone. Everything seemed to glow with an inner radiance of its own, setting him at peace.

"Is there anything else?"

His mother shook her head. "You look tired. Why don't you rest?"

"What time is it?"

"I don't know."

"Yecheil will be home soon, don't you think?"

"Rest."

He sat by the stove with his eyes closed, warming his toes, and at first, when the kiss brushed his cheek, and he awoke with the narrow, bearded face almost touching his own, he was sure it was all a dream.

"You're back!" he cried, throwing his arms about

his cousin's neck and kissing him on the mouth. "Is it really you? What time is it? Have I been sleeping again? Where's Mama?"

"She's gone out."

"Shopping?"

"Yes."

"Papa too?"

Yecheil nodded, drawing up a chair, and the boy smiled. "How wonderful! Were they surprised? What will they buy, did they say?"

"A whitefish."

"No herring?"

"Not that I know of. Just a whitefish. Why?"

"But that's just the appetizer. What else?"

"The usual. Potatoes."

"That's probably for the *kugel.*" He clapped his hands with excitement. "And?"

"That's all."

"You can tell me now. What is it? I know anyway. A chicken. Isn't that it? . . . No? What then? Of course! A brisket. I forgot. Papa likes a brisket better than a chicken any day. Not a brisket either? Then what? . . . Why do you keep shaking your head?"

"Because I don't understand. Where do you think we'd get the money to buy a brisket or a chicken?"

"Then how much money *did* you get?"

"A ruble."

"For all of the whips?"

"All of them?" Yecheil laughed. "Ah, I see. You've had a dream. No." He took the boy's hand. "I was lucky to be able to sell two. It took me all morning to sell two to the stable on Kruvelska Street for fifty kopeks apiece."

The boy stared at him without comprehending. "And that's the only place you went?"

"No."

"Then where else?"

"Let's see. Ah. Danilovichevska. The stable on the corner. But they were closed."

"And that's all?"

"That's all."

"And Zlota Street?" asked the boy.

"Is that what you thought?"

"It's only what you said you were going to do."

"No."

"You did so. Ask Mama. Last night you said the groom on Zlota Street would buy all of your whips."

"And he would, if I say so, yes."

"Then why didn't you go?"

"Because," said Yecheil, "when I do, the money makes no difference. It . . ." he hesitated, tugging at his beard. "How can I explain?"

"No, there's no need. I understand."

"What's this? Before the Sabbath? Tears?"

"No tears. No."

"Where are you going?"

"Just inside. It's late. If you don't want to be late at the *mikveh,* you ought to go."

"Wait."

"For what? I told you. I understand. It's all right. It was childish of me. You had to say something."

"I told the truth."

"No. But what's so terrible? I don't mind. I know it's not your fault."

"Blow your nose."

"You mustn't speak to me as a child any more. I told you. I understand. It took me a long time, but I do. Yesterday, it was just what I told Mama. It isn't anybody's fault. There's just nothing else that any of us can do."

"No."

"Then what?"

"Get your coat," said Yecheil.

"Why?"

"Here. Button up. Button up. That's it. Haven't you got any gloves? Your hands are red. Where did I leave my whips?"

"Where are we going?"

"For the love of heaven. Will you please wipe your nose?"

In front of the tailor shop, the boy stumbled in the ankle-deep snow. "Don't stop! Don't stop!" Yecheil shouted, catching him up under the arm, but he stumbled again. Warming himself by the fire, one of the sentries laughed and shouted something, but the words were carried away by the wind that drove the falling snow down the length of the street. The soldier yelled again and shook his fist, but they had reached the corner. With the low, gray sky and the air filled with swirling flakes, the Prospect was almost in darkness, as though the sun had already set. Here and there a yellow oil lamp burned in a frosted window. They crossed the wide street and headed west. Ghostly figures, sheeted in snow, glided silently by them; a peasant in a fur cap, bent under a load of wood, a man in a military overcoat, with his head shrouded in a hood. As far as the boy could judge, they went west again, along a narrow maze of streets that he had never seen before, between red-brick factory buildings whose smoking chimneys blackened the snow with soot. It began to snow even harder, in thick wet flakes that clung to the eyelashes and stuck to their clothes. Yecheil held the boy by the hand. The wind howled in his ears. Half blinded, unable to see anything but the dim, white shape before him, his thoughts became confused.

"West, or east?" he wondered. "Is that the river? Where is he taking me?" He lost all sense of time.

They struggled on until the boy's body was numb and it required all of his will to put one foot in front of the other, and it wasn't until the wind had abruptly died away that he realized that they had entered an enclosed court of a block of flats, and halted once and for all. He wiped his face. There was an outside stairway, with a row of dripping icicles hanging from the iron rail, and to his right, almost directly before him, he could see a double wooden door.

"Your honor!" cried Yecheil, in Polish, but using the Russian form of address. "Your honor, let us in!"

"Who is it?" came a muffled voice.

"Your honor, open the door!" said Yecheil, pounding on it with his fist.

The door slid back, throwing the gleam of a lantern on the drifted snow.

"Who is it?" repeated a man in a leather apron. The falling snow obscured his face. ". . . The Jew! Don't tell me. The Jew has changed his mind." He gave a short, delighted laugh. "Who's that?"

"Only my cousin," said Yecheil. "Won't your honor let us in?"

"Come in. Come in, by all means."

"Thank his honor for his kindness," said Yecheil.

"I thank your honor," said the boy.

The huge room, echoing to his voice, smelled of rotting hay and manure. When his eyes became accustomed to the flickering light of a lantern hanging on the wall, he could see a shadowy row of wooden stalls in the rear, with horses in them. The man before him, thick-set and round-faced, with wide nostrils and tiny, glittering eyes, scratched the shaven nape of his neck with an iron curry comb and grinned.

"What'd I tell you? Didn't I say you'd be back? You don't get an offer like mine every day."

"It's true," said Yecheil. "Your honor is very kind." The snow in his beard and eyebrows was beginning to melt in huge glistening drops.

"Eh? Well? Then you agree? How many is it to be? How many whips have you got there? Ten? Twelve? I tell you what. I'll take them all. What do you want for all of them?" He jingled the coins in the pocket of his apron. "Six rubles? Seven?"

"Seven rubles?" asked David in astonishment.

"Look at him, will you? Will you just have a look at that boy!" laughed the groom, jingling the coins again. "You like the sound of that, eh? Eh? . . . Why, he's positively watering at the mouth. . . . Tsk, tsk. A real Jew. So young, imagine that, and already a Jew." He held his sides and roared with laughter. In the rear, one of the horses stomped its hooves.

"I thought—to celebrate the Sabbath," stammered David, feeling himself flush to the roots of his hair.

"Of course. Of course. What's it to be? You can tell me, after all. What are you going to buy with all that money? . . . I know! A suckling, eh? Eh? Isn't that it? A roast suckling, brown and tender, with an apple in its mouth. . . ."

"Oh, no . . . that is . . . no, no suckling, your honor," said the boy. "We're not allowed . . ."

The man threw back his head and roared again.

The restless horse brushed its flanks against the stall. The wall shook and the swinging lanterns made their shadows on the floor sway one way and the other in a slowly diminishing arc.

"Well, what do you say?" said the groom, turning to Yecheil.

". . . Ten whips."

"As many as you like."

"That's ten pulls."

"You know the offer," he said, shifting the comb from hand to hand. "Take it or leave it. Well?"

"Pulls?" asked David.

"Make up your mind. I haven't got all day."

"Pulls? I don't understand," repeated the boy.

"His honor has been kind enough to offer to buy a whip for every time I allow him to pull my beard," said Yecheil.

It was some kind of joke. The boy was sure of it. He looked from one to the other. The groom, grinning, cleared his throat with a curious, embarrassed air, and Yecheil was smiling too, with his mouth twisted to one side.

"Yes or no?" asked the groom. "I've got work to do. You're wasting my time."

"I know. I apologize, and, if I may, I must again express my thanks to your honor," said Yecheil, bowing low from the waist.

The man took a step forward. "Then it's yes?"

"Ah, I must . . . I . . . no," said Yecheil. "No. Perhaps. . . . No, not today."

"No, eh?" said the groom.

Still bent, without raising his eyes, and with a wave of his arm, a gesture for the boy to follow him, Yecheil began to turn toward the partly opened door.

"No?"

The turn was completed. He had reached the threshold and straightened up, but it was too late. The curry comb clanged to the floor and the thick, muscled arm of the groom shot out, all in one motion, one sound, as though an iron bolt had been shot to bar the door. The boy heard the horse snort and stomp again in the stall, and a quick, sharp intake of breath, a little grunt. Crouching down, with his back against the wall and his arms in front of his face, he saw only a part of what happened. He only caught a glimpse of the groom's face, the flaring nostrils and little eyes. There was no malice in them, or even amusement, or delight; a certain dullness, rather, a matter of factness that frightened him even more. It was as though he were beating a horse. Holding Yecheil's face up by the beard, his right fist rose and fell. "No, eh? No, eh? No?" The horse was growing more excited. Again the lantern swayed and the shadows moved back and forth. A whinny filled the air, and the sound of splintering wood.

"Yes, yes," the groom muttered under his breath. "In a minute, damn you. One minute more." David shut his eyes. "No, eh?" Then there was a silence. He was aware that the groom had grabbed him by the left arm, wrenching his shoulder. Then he was being dragged across the floor toward the door.

They sat for a time in the court, underneath the stairway. The icicles were beginning to melt. It had stopped snowing at last and the darkening sky was beginning to clear, showing ragged patches of yellow and blue in the east, and an occasional ray of the declining sun. From the street came the creak of an ungreased axle as a horse-drawn cart went by.

"You heard him," said Yecheil. "Seven rubles for a few pulls of the beard. . . ." He spoke with difficulty. His lower lip was slit at the corner. His cheek was bruised and his left eye swollen almost shut. "Ah, I can see it. . . . You still don't understand."

"You refused," said David. "If you refuse, then why do you come?"

"Because he gives me a choice. . . . Yes. . . . Don't you see?" He dabbed at his lip and spat blood.

"Sit down."

"No, no, it's nothing. . . . And why? For that very reason . . . because I have a choice. I refuse . . . it . . . how shall I say it? I . . . och!"

"Sit down and put some snow on your face."

"Listen to me!" The shut eye, as though he were winking, gave his face a peculiar, sly expression. "Listen. . . . You see, you were wrong. . . . There's always a choice to be made." Again he spat blood and began to cough violently. "Remember that," he said, gasping for breath. "Remember that and rejoice. . . . Rejoice. . . . Praise Him. . . . God provides."

The Prisoner

In the winter of 1906, when my father was fourteen years old, the Russian military barracks on Mila Street in Warsaw was turned into a prison, and its iron gate, with its crest of the two-headed eagle, became known in Polish as "The Portal of Tears" because it was from here that those prisoners convicted by military tribunal of having taken part in the uprising the year before were sent to the penal camps in Siberia, or the mines.

As it happened, late one night after the first of the year, one of the prison's turnkeys, a Pole who had been bribed by the congregation of the neighborhood synagogue, came across the street and knocked three times on my grandfather's door.

"Who is it?" the boy called out.

"Open up."

"Who's there?"

"Ha Malach," the Pole had been taught to reply to identify himself—in Hebrew, "the angel," literally "the messenger," one who has been sent from God—so that when the boy opened the door, in that instant before

the light from the inside illuminated the man's face, the dark figure in the overcoat and fur cap set his heart to pounding, and made him catch his breath.

"Is his honor at home?"

"Who?"

"Your father, quick! Where is he?"

"In the kitchen," the boy told him, coming to himself at last. "Come in." By the time he had glanced up and down the street to make sure no one was watching, then locked up, and closed the door to the bedroom where his mother was asleep, the two men were whispering together over the red-hot stove.

"What is it, Papa? What does he want?" the boy asked, although he already knew. It was a meeting that had been arranged months before, at the beginning of the summer, in the eventuality that a Jew would be imprisoned at the barracks.

"Go to bed, David," his father told him.

"But what's he say? Have they really got a Jew? Will you go and see him?"

"We'll see," said the old man. The Pole raised his head in the flickering candlelight and grinned.

"*Ha Malach.* . . . A messenger from God who wears a fur cap and a scraggly mustache that reaches to his chin. Is that possible?" the boy wondered the next morning as he wound his philacteries around his arm to pray. Through the frosted window above his bed he could see the sentries marching up and down.

He tried to picture the Jewish prisoner in his cell. Israel in Egypt, Joseph in the dungeons of the Pharaoh: all those he had read about who had suffered torture and martyrdom for the Sanctification of the Name ran through his mind. He felt exhausted and feverish. All night long, he had dreamed of piles of smoldering faggots and bloody whips. Supposing, just supposing—and anything might happen—he would be called upon one day to help a captive. Would he prove worthy of the holy obligation?

"*Hineni,*" he prayed aloud in Hebrew. "Here I am. Lord God of my Fathers, Master of the Universe, do with me what you will."

"Is it true? Are you going to the barracks?" he asked his father at breakfast.

"On Friday, yes. He wants a blanket and some food."

"But what about the guards?" asked the boy, buttering his bread.

"The guards can be bribed."

"For how much?"

"Fifty rubles."

"Fifty rubles! Where will you get fifty rubles?"

"Where do you think? From the synagogue, of course."

And so it was. Night after night, for the remainder of the week, the old man passed the hat in the vestibule of the synagogue up the street.

"Five kopeks?" he shouted at Rabinowitz the cobbler. "Five miserable kopeks are all you can spare for a scholar who once studied Torah with the Sage of Kotsk?"

"The Sage of where?" asked Jacobson the hatmaker.

"Yes, it's true. With Rabbi Getz of Kotsk himself," said Bunem the sexton, who cleared his throat, and in his high, piping voice read aloud from a letter that the rabbi had addressed to the whole congregation:

". . . Is it true what I have heard? Avram Shulmann? Condemned to seven years? Surely our brothers in Warsaw will find it in their hearts to do whatever they can for one whom I had once hoped would teach the Law in my place when I am gone. . . ."

"Condemned for seven years?" repeated the cobbler.

"Yes, and to the mines! To the lead mines, Jews, do you hear?" cried Bunem, snatching the hat and shoving it under Rabinowitz's nose.

"But for what? What's he done?" the boy wanted to know. In the hubbub, nobody answered. It didn't make sense. Not if the prisoner had studied with the Sage of Kotsk. Not unless . . . The boy gaped at his father counting the coins in the hat. Unless—may God forbid—he had denied the Almighty, and become an Anarchist or a Socialist of some kind, one of those wild young men who threw bombs at the police, and last year erected barricades on Market Street.

There were all sorts of rumors about him, whispered in the back of the synagogue, or on the steps, outside; that he had been a Kabbalist, an ascetic mystic, who had been forced to leave Kotsk after a young girl, practically a child, had hanged herself in the House of Study.

"Nonsense," said the cantor, after services on Thursday night, when the fifty rubles had been collected. He was a half-blind old man who swore that the sister of the cantor of Kotsk, his wife's cousin, had written him the truth. The prisoner had gone mad after a pogrom in the town some years ago, and tearing off his clothes in the market place, literally foaming at the mouth, had denied God, and attacked the rabbi with his nails and teeth.

"Stark raving mad," said the cantor. "It's a fact."

His pale-blue eyes, covered by a milky film, sent a shudder up and down the boy's spine.

When his father finally returned from the barracks just before sundown the next night, the boy was completely bewildered. "What happened? Did you see him?" he asked.

"Yes, I saw him," said the old man.

"What did he say?"

"He thanked me for the blanket and the roast."

"Is that all?"

"What else did you expect?"

"But you were there the whole afternoon."

The old man washed his hands and slipped into a clean kaftan for the Sabbath meal.

"Eat, Mikhal," his wife coaxed him at the table. "The soup will get cold."

"What? Oh yes, the soup," he replied, putting down his spoon to rise abruptly from the table and take his Bible down from the shelf.

"What is it, Papa? What's the matter?" asked the boy.

"Nothing."

But it was a lie. For half the night, until he fell into a dreamless sleep, the boy heard him pace the floor, pausing now and then to mutter some passage in Hebrew under his breath. In the morning, he was seated in front of the kitchen window, staring at the huge dark building across the street, with the Bible closed in his lap.

"What did he say?" the boy repeated. "Has he become a Socialist? Is that the trouble?"

"Who told you that?"

"Is it true?"

"Yes," said the old man, absently winding one of his graying earlocks around a finger.

"Then he doesn't believe in God?"

"Oh yes, he believes." The old man suddenly burst out laughing, after staring at his son for a moment, open-mouthed.

The boy couldn't figure it out. The following Tuesday night, the Pole knocked on the door again, and insisted on seeing the old man, who had already gone to bed. They spoke in the kitchen behind a closed door.

"Impossible. . . . There's nothing I can do," the boy heard his father say.

"Your honor . . . mines . . ." said the Pole, and with a squeaking of a chair along the floor, and more words, the door was suddenly flung open, and the two men appeared. Once again, the figure of the man in the fur cap with the long mustache filled the boy with the same mysterious feeling as before—a mixture of exaltation and dread that dried up his mouth.

"Where're you going?" he called out.

"He wants to see me."

"At this hour?"

"I'll be back as soon as I can. Tell your mother," said the old man, putting on his shoes. On the kitchen table, lying open, was the Bible that he had been reading and rereading for the last few days. Bound in peeling red leather, with a silver clasp, the book was very old. The boy lit another candle and bent down to examine the yellowed pages. A passage from Hosea had been underlined by the imprint of his father's fingernail. In the wavering light, the words seemed to dance in front of his eyes.

"'. . . I will be like a lion to them,'" he read aloud. 'Like a leopard will I lurk by the way. I will meet them like a bear who has lost her cubs, and tear open their breasts. There will I devour them like a lion. Like a wild beast will I rend them. . . .'"

What did it mean? It was a passage from the Bible the boy had never understood. This was the Lord of the Universe who was speaking, the God of Mercy who was comparing Himself to a wild animal stalking his prey. The fire in the stove went out. Shivering, the boy fell asleep with his head on his arm.

For the next two days, his father shuffled around the house in his felt slippers as if he had taken ill. Weary and distracted, with a drawn face, and dazed eyes, it was only when he recited his prayers that he seemed conscious of what he was doing. The boy had never seen him pray with such fervor. In the evenings, particularly, just before he went to bed, he finished with trembling lips and tears in his eyes. The Bible remained open on the kitchen table. "Impossible," he muttered through clenched teeth, reading the same passage again and again. "Impossible. . . . What does he want from me?"

On Friday morning, he called his son to his room.

"Tell Bunem I want to see him," he said in a hoarse voice.

"What about me, Papa? Isn't there anything I can do?"

"Bunem," the old man insisted, and an hour or so later, when the boy had brought the sexton home, he lingered in the room in order to hear what his father had to say.

"Sit down. Sit down." He waved his hand. "A little brandy? No? Then sit a minute. I . . ." He lowered his eyes and the color rushed into his wrinkled cheeks. "You must . . . I . . . You must do me a favor," he went on at last.

"Of course."

"Yes. . . . Very special. You must make him understand. I talk and I talk, but it doesn't do any good. He thinks . . . I have a message for him, for our friend, do you understand?"

"A message?" repeated the sexton in his high voice.

"You must tell him that I'm very sorry, but there's absolutely nothing I can do. Will you remember that?"

"I don't understand."

"It's very simple. All you have to do is repeat what I'm telling you."

"When?"

"This afternoon. I promised that I'd return today, but it's useless. . . . Worse. You must go instead. Stanislaw will be here at five."

"Stanislaw?" said Bunem, rising to his feet.

"The turnkey. What's the matter with you?"

"B-but that's impossible," the sexton stammered. "W-what I mean to say is that I'd like to, of course—you know I would—but it's absolutely out of the question. A message! Are you mad? What about the police? What would happen to me if they found out I was giving information to a political prisoner?"

"The message is personal. You have nothing to fear from that."

"That's all very well for you to say with a grown son, practically a man who can look after himself if anything should happen to you—may God forbid! But what about my daughters? Three helpless girls. Who would look after them if anything happened to me? No. For their sake, I can't even think of taking such a chance." He shook his head. "B-but I'll tell you what I'll do. They can cook, those girls. Especially Leah. A roast chicken, how's that? And with potato pancakes. What do you say to that, eh?" He backed away toward the door. "And out of my own pocket. A whole roast chicken, a Sabbath feast for him to remember for the rest of his life, no matter what they do to him. Well? What do you say?"

"Tell Rabinowitz and Jacobson I want to see them," the old man answered, shutting his eyes.

He might as well have saved his breath. No one came except Leah, a good half a head taller than her father, with a deeper voice, and a prominent adam's apple like an adolescent boy, who brought the promised chicken and pancakes wrapped in a greasy newspaper. When she left, the boy waited in the kitchen for the turnkey's knock on the door.

"No, I won't go," his father repeated to himself under his breath, wandering around the house in his slippers.

"But what about the food?" the boy asked.

"The food?"

"The Pole will only eat it himself. It's not fair. The Sabbath is coming."

"The food, yes," said his father, sitting down with his head in his hands.

"Let me take it," said the boy.

"That's out of the question."

"Why? The guards have been bribed. It's perfectly safe. What would they want with me?"

"No," said his father.

There were three knocks on the door. Before his father had a chance to say anything more, the boy grabbed the greasy package from the table and ran into the hall.

"What is it now? Who are you?" asked the prisoner when the turnkey had locked the boy in the cell.

As far as he could make out, he was in a cellar of some kind, in one of the rooms off a long corridor with a vaulted ceiling that ran beneath a wing of the barracks that faced the inner court. "Who's there?" the prisoner repeated, with a rattle of chains. It was too dark for the boy to see his face. Without a window in the cell, it was already night in here, bitter cold, and yet stifling from a stench of excrement that had first stunned the boy when he and the Pole were only half-way down the last flight of stairs.

"I . . . That is, my father couldn't come," said the boy.

"Who?"

"My father. He said . . . I've brought you some food instead."

"How nice. That's very thoughtful. Thank you very much."

"Don't mention it. Good *Shabbos*," said the boy, handing him the package.

"By all means. And to you, too."

The boy's eyes were gradually becoming accustomed to the dark. He could see that the prisoner's head was shaved, cropped to the skull, and he was wearing a peculiar vest, like a uniform, with black and gray horizontal stripes.

"My father sends you a message," the boy went on.

"Oh?"

"He wanted me to tell you that he can't help you. There's nothing he can do."

"I see."

"But he says that he's very sorry."

"Yes, I understand. Will you thank him for me just the same?"

"Of course."

"Good."

Again there was the rattle of chains. All at once the boy realized that the prisoner's wrists were chained to a thick leather strap around his waist. He squatted down on a pile of straw. Was there enough play in the fetters to enable the man to eat, the boy wondered.

"Can I help?" he asked, kneeling down. The prisoner shook his head. His prayers, of course, thought the boy. Before he ate, he would want to say the blessing. Maybe there was even a special prayer for the redemption of the captive that Rabbi Getz had taught him.

"What's your name?" the prisoner asked, working the iron bands down his forearms and rubbing his wrists.

"David."

"Then David, do you know why I'm here?"

"I think so. You're a Socialist."

"Do you know what that means?"

"I'm not sure. Did you throw a bomb?"

"Oh no, much worse. I wrote a book."

"About what?"

"About a lot of things. About a pogrom, a little girl, and the class struggle. Do you know what the class struggle is?"

"No."

"It's a war. A war against the Tzar, and the Cossacks, and the police. Against all the people who make pogroms. In a way, you know, I'm a soldier. But it's your war too."

"If you say so," said the boy.

"But it is. It's everybody's war, whether they like it or not, and it will go on and on for a long time to come. That's the rule of life. Can you keep a secret?"

"Yes."

"Would you like to do something for me? Something very important?"

"If I can."

"Do you know where Iron Street is?"

"I think so."

"Do you think you could find Number Twelve for me?"

"I could try. Why?"

"Shhh! Listen!"

"I don't hear anything."

"Yes, shhh!" the prisoner whispered. "The turnkey will be back in a moment, so there's no time to explain. Will you go to Number Twelve Iron Street on Sunday morning and deliver a very important message for me?"

"Yes," said the boy.

"Without telling another soul?"

"If that's what you want."

"That's very important. You must be careful. I'm

relying on you because there's no one else I can ask."

"I understand."

"Good. At Number Twelve, you must knock three times on the porter's door, and a girl will answer, a Polish girl, with very blonde hair and blue eyes. Her hair is almost white. You can't mistake her."

"What do I tell her?"

"You must say that you have a message from her cousin who says that he's going away to the country at the end of next week, probably Friday. Can you remember all of that?"

"Yes."

"Fine. But you must promise to be as careful as you can. It's very dangerous. If anyone else answers the door, for example, you must say that you've made a mistake and go away."

"I'll remember."

"Good boy," said the prisoner. "Now tell me something."

"What?"

"How old are you?"

"Fourteen."

"Really? How strange. She was almost fourteen too."

"Who?"

"Yes, just about the same age. How strange," said the prisoner, in a distracted, dreamy voice, as the key turned suddenly in the lock, and the Pole threw open the door, lighting up the cell with the hurricane lamp he held in his hand.

The boy gave a start. The prisoner's face seemed to leap out of the dark. Because of his shaved head, his ears stuck out, and his eyes looked enormous. He blinked painfully, and tried to raise his hands, rattling his chains.

"I gave him your message," the boy told his father when he got home. "He said to thank you."

The old man nodded and looked away.

On Sunday morning, the boy woke to the peal of church bells, and stumbled into the empty kitchen for a glass of tea. Iron Street, Number Twelve. A blonde Polish girl, with blue eyes. What was she like, he wondered, tip-toeing to the front door. Did she actually smoke like some of the girls—students, Socialists, God only knew what—whom he often saw in the cafés on Marshalkovska Street, puffing away on yellow Russian cigarettes? Was she also wanted by the police for writing books? And if they caught her, would they shave off her hair?

"David?"

"I'll be back in a little while, Papa."

"Come in here a moment. Where are you going at this hour?"

"Nowhere, Papa. Just out for a walk."

"At this hour? Come in here, I say. . . ."

The boy did as he was told. His mother was still in bed. Already dressed and preparing to begin his morning prayers, the old man questioned his son again. On the dresser beside him, bound in black, was a prayer book with the morning service containing the words from the Psalm that the boy knew by heart: " . . . deliver my soul, O God, from lying lips and from a deceitful tongue. . . ."

"Well?" said the old man, waiting for an answer.

The boy told him the truth. "But I was doing it for you, too, after all. . . ."

"What are you talking about?" said his father.

"Didn't he ask you to go to Iron Street?"

"Is that what he told you? Where's my coat?" the old man shouted.

"Where are you going?"

"My coat!"

The boy followed him outside. It had begun to snow. They crossed the street, went through the gate past the yawning sentries and down the cellar stairs, into the dark, vaulted corridor, where the astonished Pole dropped an armful of straw to open up the prisoner's cell.

"Yes, what of it?" he admitted to the old man. "I found out when I was to be deported, and the Party had to be informed."

"At the risk of a child's life?"

"Yes."

"And if he'd been caught?"

"Then whatever he would have suffered would have been meaningful, at least; to some end."

"The Revolution?"

"Yes."

"Which alone can give meaning to human suffering?"

"By making an end to it, yes," said the prisoner. His face was turned away, hidden by darkness, but from the sound of his voice, the boy had the impression that his eyes were tightly shut.

"I don't understand, Papa. What does he mean?"

"Tell him," said the prisoner. "He has a right to judge for himself."

The old man remained silent.

"Then listen to me," the prisoner went on, grabbing the boy by the arm. "I told you, it's a war . . . for you . . . for the children, the little girl, remember? Fourteen years old, your age, with long black hair. . . . When I was studying Torah with Rabbi Getz at Kotsk, there was a pogrom. One Sunday, after church, the peasants went mad. The police gave them brandy. Yes, the police. On orders from the District Commissioner himself. There was a drought that season, and the crops had failed. The peasants were starving. 'Turn them on the Jews' was the order. The police gave them brandy, and they went mad, like wild animals, and began murdering the Jews wherever they could find them.

. . . The rabbi and I hid in the attic of the House of Study where all the old prayer books were stored, piles of them, loose pages by the thousands, turning yellow, gnawed by mice and crumbling to dust. We buried ourselves alive under books, listening to the screams. . . . I raised my head to the window.

" 'Don't look,' the rabbi tells me. 'Shut your eyes, my son, and pray. . . .'

"But I look just the same. I can't tear my eyes away, so I see what they do to a fourteen-year-old girl, the daughter of the Jew who owns the mill on the edge of town. One of them sits on her head, while they take turns. All told, there are six of them, and when they're finished, and see that she's still alive, still fully conscious, they cut open her belly with a sickle, and stuff it with goose feathers from a pillow they've looted from a house across the street. . . .

" 'Don't look,' the rabbi tells me, 'don't look.' But it was too late. I had seen everything . . . the whole truth."

"The truth?" the boy repeated.

"It's a war," said the prisoner, rattling his chains. "A war."

When the old man and the boy left the cell, the Pole followed them to the gate.

"Can I help your honor?" he asked, shivering in his cotton blouse. The boy had become accustomed to him. He was now just an ordinary man, with eyes watering from the cold. Yet, because of the falling snow, there was something mysterious about the whole scene. It was as if the invisible were on the verge of becoming visible before the boy's eyes. Yes, that was it, exactly, thought the boy. It was because of the air. The thick, feathery snowflakes imparted a visible depth to the hitherto dimensionless air—something the boy had never noticed before. For some reason, the awareness frightened him.

"Go home, David," said his father. "Tell Mama I'll be back as soon as I can."

He walked off, through the gate, heading toward the Prospect. To Iron Street? The boy never found out. And did the Pole, too, suspect something of the kind? He wiped his running eyes. Who could tell what he was thinking? He came to the house twice more, on Monday and Thursday of the following week, to try and persuade the old man to see the prisoner for the last time.

"What does he want from me now?" he asked, closing his Bible.

"He says your honor already knows."

"Then I can do nothing for him. No, nothing," he repeated to his son. "You needn't look at me like that. There's nothing that either you or I or anyone can do for him any more, and that's all there is to it."

But on Thursday afternoon, as the boy knew he would, the old man relented. He and the boy followed the Pole through the gate for the last time, and down the steps to the cellar.

"It's happened again," said the prisoner, rising to his feet.

"When?"

"Twice so far this week. On Monday, and again this morning. And it's getting worse."

"How do you mean?"

"How can I explain? It's . . . The feeling is getting stronger, somehow, and it lasts longer. For minutes at a time."

"What's he mean, Papa? What's he talking about?" the boy asked.

"This morning, for example," said the prisoner. "I was lying here, thinking about the mines. That once I was there, everything would be all right. . . . That is, there are Party cells out there, you know, even classes, and lectures from the Comrades, after a fashion, a whole organization under their very noses, so that you can carry on with the work that has to be done, and one needn't give up hope. . . . The struggle goes on. . . ."

"And then what?" the old man interrupted him.

"I told you. Like before. The light. . . . It . . . It was breakfast time, and the turnkey opened the door to give me the bread. . . . I . . . It's hard to describe. His lamp, you know. For a moment, it blinds me. Afterwards, it takes a minute or so to get used to the dark again. . . . That is, to see in the dark. Generally, I can see in here very well, but when he shines a light . . . Anyway, most of the time, I'm blind for a minute or two, and then it passes, and that's all there is to it. But this morning, like Monday, and, as I've told you, three or four times before, it seemed more than just dark, more than just the absence of light, as if the darkness were a substance itself. . . . Yes . . . The same, as solid—or, rather, as fluid, or maybe gaseous, as that stone wall, for example; yes, as real as that, or the oak door. . . . Yet not exactly solid, either, or even like a gas—real, but not material at all. . . ."

He paused, and then went on in a whisper. "No, maybe that's not the right word. It . . . I shut my eyes, tight, but it didn't do any good. When I opened them, it was worse. Darker, somehow, dissolving everything, the stone and the wood, or, rather, as if the dark and the stone and the wood were all the same. . . . Exactly. As if everything were part of everything else. . . . The floor, too, and the straw, and then my legs, my left one first, and then the other, and my hands, and the chains on my wrists, all dissolving, but . . ."

"And then?" said the old man.

"Just like before, the same as before, I told you. . . . Everything on the verge of becoming a part of everything else, and trembling, vibrating like flecks of dust in a shaft of sunlight but, at the same time, terribly distinct. By this time, I could see again, perfectly:

the straw on the floor, even the dirt under my fingernails, each and every straw, and every one perfectly distinct, and . . . significant. Meaningful, each one, every straw on the floor, the way it lay, either lengthwise or crosswise, meaningful and significant. It seemed right and good—morally good, you understand—that each one should be the way it was—perfect. In perfect order. . . . No. Much more than that. There are no words to describe it. The joy, the inexpressible joy. . . ."

"And then?" repeated the old man.

"Like before. Myself. My own body. Even the chains. Solid, material, and perfect, but then again, on the verge of dissolving too, trembling, like everything else, so that I had to hold myself in—my breath, with all the strength I had. . . . No, not my breath so much. More than that, much more. . . . My *ruach*. The Hebrew word describes it best. The breath and the spirit together. . . . I had to hold it back with all the strength I had, because it too seemed on the verge of being—becoming part of the rest . . . dissolved . . . with joy. If I let go, it would rush out, and merge . . . roar out. Roar with joy. . . ."

"And so?"

"Joy? How could I? What about her? The child, I mean. Joy? No. Not if I could still think, feel . . . indignation. But when I thought of her, it wasn't any good. Oh, I could remember it all, vividly: the dusty street, the peasant with the sunburned neck who held the sickle, squinting from the sun that gleamed on the blade, the girl herself, her foot, with the shoe untied. . . .

"Yes, I could remember it all, but it was like the straws. The straws, do you hear? All in order. The sickle, the untied shoe—in order, significant, meaningful. . . . More. Good. . . . No, holy."

"Let go. Let go of my arm," said the old man. "Let me go, I tell you. What do you want from me?"

"Make Him stop, why don't you? Tell me how to make Him stop," the prisoner cried in a stifled voice. "Hasn't He done enough? Why can't He let me alone?"

"Who, Papa? Who's he talking about? I don't understand," said the boy.

NOW: ISRAEL

The Blessing

WHEN Rabbi Levinsky finally left, it was late in the afternoon. Yitshaak went out onto the balcony to watch the old man going home: a solitary, graceless figure, dressed in a long black coat that flapped about his knees as he walked, with one hand thrust behind him, and the other pulling at his beard. The road lined by eucalyptus trees led uphill. From time to time the old man paused to catch his breath. Even on the balcony, the air was stifling, redolent of plaster and the exhaust fumes of cars. The long tapering leaves of the trees, shaped like knife blades, were covered with dust. The heated air shimmered above the red-tiled roofs of the houses on top of the hill. Beyond them, to the west, beyond the highway to Haifa, and shining between the gaps in the sand dunes, the inert Mediterranean reflected the pale-blue sky.

On the crest of the hill, Levinsky looked back. Yitshaak drew away from the railing, but it was too late; the old man had seen him and, with a gesture that was unmistakable in spite of the distance, he reproved him again with a shake of his head. Then he went on his way. The road turned left. Yitshaak watched until he was hidden by the row of whitewashed houses and the dusty trees.

Standing there, facing the road, Yitshaak could see the grammar school that served the children of the neighborhood. It was here that his son had been enrolled in the third grade before he had been taken ill. Yitshaak put his hand to his forehead, shielding his eyes from the sun, in an effort to see into the classroom where the boy had studied. It was on the first floor, north, in the corner of the building, but there was nothing to be seen inside. The window was dark.

He took a deep breath. Since three-thirty, when he had returned home from the hospital at Petach Tikva, he had longed only to be left alone with his wife, Nira, who had taken to her bed as soon as she had heard the news. Now, with Levinsky gone, he was frightened at the thought of it. He was grateful that Esther, her aunt, was with her. Not that it really made any difference; he was going to have to tell them both what he had decided. In a way, Esther was responsible. He thought back to earlier in the afternoon and pictured her standing in the doorway when she had first heard about the boy, with one plump arm raised, and those disquieting eyes becoming suddenly brilliant with tears. For an instant, without catching the words, the sound of her voice echoed in his ears. Then there was the silence with a voice of its own—a faint buzzing that oppressed him even more. His gaze returned to the school. A little yellow Arab dog, casting an enormous shadow in the light of the declining sun, was crossing the yard with its nose to the ground.

"Yitshaak?"

It was Esther from the living room. "Yitshaak? Yitshaak, where are you?" He gave himself a moment more—until the dog reached the corner of the building, and then went to face her in the open door.

"There you are. Where is he? Levinsky's gone?"

"A few minutes ago."

"Without saying good-by?"

As always, her glance made him uneasy. He wasn't sure why. Her irises were pale-blue, almost colorless, clear and untroubled, like a child's. This afternoon was the first time he had ever seen her cry. Maybe that was why. She had been in the country for twelve years, the only member of her immediate family to survive the concentration camps. Belsen, a trek across the Alps in winter and on foot, a year's internment on Cyprus, and now the shabby rented room in Ramat Gan where she lived alone, without complaint, and supported herself as a dressmaker's assistant—her curious, serene eyes, set in that plump, aging face, revealed nothing of what she had seen.

"What about tomorrow?" she asked. "What time does the service start?"

"Early. Eight-thirty."

"That's a good idea. The earlier the better. We'll get Nira back here before it gets too hot."

"I guess so."

"From Petach Tikva? Why not? It won't take more than a half hour to get home. If the service starts promptly at eight-thirty, we'll be back here by eleven at the latest. What about the hired cars?"

"What about them?"

"How many are you going to have?"

"One. Why?"

"I thought so. That's not enough. That's only enough for the four of us—Levinsky, you, me, and Nira. What about Zvi and the Rosens?" They were clerks with whom Yitshaak worked in the safe-deposit department of the bank on Allemby Road.

"Zvi'll drive himself," he said.

"Has he got a car?"

"A Jeep."

"Wonderful. I didn't know. Who else? How about Lani? What's her name? You know. Nira's friend from school. Oh, you know who I mean. The girl who married that doctor in Natanya."

"Goldman."

"That's the one."

"They're away," Yitshaak said. "They went away on vacation."

"Where?"

"I don't know. Nira may know."

"She's sleeping. You can ask her when she gets up. We'll send them a telegram. Would you like me to call the others?"

"If you like."

"I'll call them from the pharmacy when I go shopping. Oh. That reminds me. Something else. It's important. I almost forgot."

"What?"

"If they all go to the cemetery, we'll have to invite them back here afterwards for something to eat."

"Yes," said Yitshaak. "I remember. The meal of condolence. . . . " It seemed so remote; all of the random memories of his religious upbringing seemed now to belong to another life; the dark Polish synagogue on Dizengoff Road with its slippery floor, the candles and fish on Friday night, the red velvet *tallis* bag that his father had given him on his thirteenth birthday. . . .

"We'll have to give them eggs or lentils to begin with," Esther said. "That's required. After that, you can have whatever you like; meat if you want. I thought maybe I'd make veal cutlets."

He shrugged; she chattered on, now and again dabbing at the sweat on her upper lip.

"What is it?" she asked. "Is anything the matter?"

"No, no, go on. I'm listening," he said, coming into the room at last and sitting himself down on the sofa with his hands on his knees.

"Did he tell you I knew his wife?"

"Who?"

"Levinsky."

"Yes. He mentioned it."

"It's a small world. I used to make all of her dresses when they lived in Ramat Gan. A lovely person. A lovely couple. I'm glad that he's the one who's going to hold the service."

Again Yitshaak shrugged. The laws of the country forbade secular funerals, and it was simply a matter of convenience to contact Levinsky who happened to live in the neighborhood.

"He's a fine old man," Esther went on. "Everyone likes him; admires him, I should say. More—depends on him. He was in Auschwitz, did you know that?"

"Yes. He mentioned that too."

"That wasn't easy for a rabbi. And not only because of the Germans, mind you. Because of our own. You can imagine what sort of a rabbi he must be if he still managed to command people's respect in a place where it was impossible to evade answering certain questions that would be asked."

"I understand."

"Do you?"

Yitshaak gazed about the room. On the coffee table, with its lace doily spread under glass, was a folded newspaper that he had bought on his way to the hospital in the morning. He took it up and began scanning the pages mechanically. It was difficult to concentrate. His eyes burned with sweat, and after a short time, even without looking up, he became aware that Esther was watching him expectantly. Rooted to the same spot in the center of the room, her transparent, inverted image—the white blur of her face and her folded arms—stared up at him from the depths of the glass. He found it impossible to speak. It was the mention of Levinsky again, the possibility that remained of hope and peace, the chance that if he spoke to the bearded old man just once more, one of his phrases, perhaps one final word that he loosed upon the desolation, would come back to roost with an olive branch. He raised the paper, frowning, and tried to resume his reading. There was an article about the necessity of conserving water during the *sharav,* the heat wave, and another, a letter to the editor from an engineer living in Jerusalem, about the dangers of exhaust fumes from cars polluting the air.

". . . greater volumes of oxides," he read, the words blurring before his eyes. This time he looked up. Quite suddenly, the light in the room seemed to have diminished. Outside, above the red roof of the school house, the pale-blue sky was becoming translucent.

"What time is it?" he asked.

"I don't know. It's getting late. I ought to go. I'll tell Zvi to drive straight to the hospital tomorrow morning. There's no sense in his coming here first."

"I'm not going," Yitshaak said.

"Where?"

"To Petach Tikva. To the funeral tomorrow. You and Nira will have to go alone."

"I don't understand."

"I'm staying at home."

"Aber ich kann nicht verstehen," she repeated, lapsing from Hebrew into German in her astonishment. "Why?"

"It was something you said."

"When?"

"When I came back from the hospital."

"I didn't say anything. What did I say?" Her eyes, clouded, suddenly cleared and widened in remembrance. With her left arm raised, unconsciously repeating the gesture she had made in the doorway, she repeated the words in a bewildered voice; the Hebrew phrase that had involuntarily escaped from her when she first heard of her nephew's death—the traditional invocation upon hearing evil news:

> "Blessed art Thou O Lord our God who art the
> true judge in Israel."

"It seemed to me—unfair," said Yitshaak. ". . . An eight-year-old boy. I told Levinsky, but he said they were part of the ritual too. I'd forgotten. I haven't been to a funeral since Papa died. Levinsky said that the same words, or words very much like them, would be repeated tomorrow, over the grave. I told him that if that were the case, I wouldn't go."

"But why? Why?"

"Don't you understand? 'A true judge. . . .' How can I have any part of that? That boy was—"

"What?"

Yitshaak shook his head.

"What was he? What? Esther repeated, leaning forward, touching the edge of the coffee table with her knees. A drop of sweat trembled from the tip of her nose. From outside, through the open door, could be heard the rumble of a truck on the road, and the faint, high drone of an airplane, coming in, or going out, over the sea.

"What? Tell me," she said, but Yitshaak remained silent. "Innocent," was what he had begun to say. In some way, he wanted to protest that his eight-year-old son, who had been condemned to suffer so and to die from cancer of the lymph nodes, had been innocent. But he said nothing because while the explanation was forming on his lips, it had suddenly occurred to him for the first time that, if anything, her own faith, like Levinsky's, had in some manner taken that very thing—the condemnation of innocence—into account. The realization had left him feeling empty and perplexed. Esther's faith, after all, had survived three and a half years in Belsen where her husband, a wealthy furrier from Berlin, had died of typhus, and from which her daughter, a girl of thirteen or fourteen at the time, had been deported to Auschwitz in a sealed boxcar and never seen again.

"No," said Esther. "It's not easy. . . . Never think, not for one moment, that one simply accepts it all once and for all, and that's all there is to it."

"Then what? Tell me."

"Ah—" She smiled, blinking her eyes rapidly in the gathering darkness. The drop of sweat still trembled from the tip of her nose.

"*Vom Tag zu Tag.*"

He stared at her without understanding.

"*Taeglich*—daily," she repeated. "*Und jeder Tag.* . . . One must struggle every day. . . ."

He pressed the heels of his palms into his eyes. No, there was something more. It wasn't simply a matter of acceptance. In time, he would come to accept the death, and even the suffering, of his son. That was only natural, almost instinctive, a process of the mind protecting itself. Even now, amidst the wheeling, fading lights in the darkness behind his tightly shut lids, he found it difficult to summon up the boy's features with exactitude. It required all of his effort just to recall the pinched face he had seen that very morning, when the doctor had lifted up the sheet on the hospital bed. The snub-nose and the wide mouth, like Nira's. The tiny mole—where was it exactly? On the left cheek, beneath the eye. . . . No. It wasn't acceptance that he rebelled against. It was something else—something which seemed to him to be monstrously humiliating. Every day, the woman before him was struggling not so much to accept the suffering inflicted upon the innocents in the camp, but to—what? Yitshaak lowered his hands. He scrutinized her: the drop of sweat had gone from her nose. Yes, he thought with astonishment, to sanctify it. She blessed God, her tormentor, and that same degradation would be required of him if he attended the funeral tomorrow. But to what end? Why? What purpose would it serve? He continued to stare at her, and, as though in answer, she raised her head, and met his questioning glance with those imperturbable eyes. . . . Reconciliation. The promise of peace.

Yitshaak stood up; the springs of the sofa creaked.

"When will you tell Nira?"

"I . . . Now," he said.

"Yitshaak?" his wife called out in a voice that was muffled by the pillow. "Who is it? Yitshaak? Is that you?"

The room was in semi-darkness. A single, broad ray of sunlight, streaming through a crack in the shutters, lit up the corner of the wall opposite the bed.

"Did I wake you?" he asked.

"No, no; what time is it?"

"Almost six."

"That late? My God. Have you had your dinner?"

"I had a late lunch," he said. "I'm not hungry."

"You mustn't be ashamed to ask Esther to make you something."

"I will, when I get hungry," he said, coming forward and sitting down as gently as he could on the edge of the bed. His wife gave him a dim smile with her wide, unpretty mouth, and turned her face toward the corner where the light was turning a deep red. A stray strand of hair, dark and stringy with sweat, lay on her cheek. She breathed deeply. Maybe she wanted to sleep some more. Yitshaak made a motion to rise.

"No, don't," she told him. Her left hand rose and fell. "Stay a little while."

"Esther wants to know if you remember Lani Goldman's address."

"Natanya. Number twelve Weizman Street."

"I thought she went away on vacation."

"She did. I forgot. They went to Naharia. I think they're staying at the Dolphin House."

"I'll tell Esther."

"Are you going to phone Lani?"

"I thought I'd send a telegram."

"Would you do me a favor?"

"What?"

"Call her, would you? Speak to her yourself. I'd like her to be with us tomorrow if she could."

"Nira?"

"What, dear?"

He reached out to grasp her left hand, but, simultaneously, she had begun a motion of her own, to brush the strand of hair away from her cheek. His empty palm fell on the bedcovers by her side.

"Where are you going?" she asked him.

"Can I get you something? A cup of tea?"

"No, no, that's all right. But you go ahead. Get yourself something to eat. You won't forget to call Lani?"

"If that's what you want."

"Yes, do," she said. "Please. Get her to come."

Esther was waiting for him, motionless against the rail. Yitshaak stood near the wall while she finished reciting the evening prayer.

"'. . . and arranges in order the stars in their watches in the firmament according to His will. . . .'"

A breeze, imperceptible at the height of the balcony, stirred the dusty leaves of the eucalyptus trees, and their dry rustling, merging now and again with her murmuring voice, was the only sound to be heard.

"'. . . and the darkness . . .'"

The breeze died away. "'. . . for ever and ever. Blessed art Thou O Lord our God who brings on the evening twilight. Amen.'"

Yitshaak was looking at the sky which was paler than the afternoon, and even more luminous. A mass of dark clouds blown in from the sea had settled above the southern horizon, and although the sun had been gone for some minutes at least, a fiery streak of opaque light lingered over the waves.

"Was Nira awake?" Esther asked.

"She wants me to call Lani."

"Did you tell her you weren't going?"

"I will. Later."

"When?"

In the last few moments, it had grown much darker still. The contours of the school and all of the houses on top of the hill had become indistinct. Here and there a pale electric light shone in a window, suspended in the dark air. The sky too, still blue, was softly lit as though from within, but the redness had faded from the clouds. Their black ragged masses drifted slowly to the east.

"When?"

The first star of the evening gleamed in the southern sky, directly above a telephone pole on the road. The drift of the clouds in the opposite direction made it appear to be racing west. Another one, much dimmer, more distant, infinitely further away in space, appeared beneath the first, and that too, because of the drift of the clouds, seemed to be racing out to sea. Yitshaak clung with both hands to the railing for support while the stars reeled above his head, and yet remained where they were, inextricably bound together above the telephone pole and the road.

"Well?"

"I . . . " Someone whistled tunelessly in the shadows beneath him. A dog barked. Soft laughter, the clatter of supper dishes drifted to him from open windows.

"Then don't tell her," Esther whispered. "Don't say anything."

"I must."

"Not if you go."

"I can't."

"Go."

"I can't," he said. "Don't you think I would if I could?"

He had turned to face her. With her head raised and partly hidden in the shadow of the wall to her right, she answered without looking at him,

"Yes."

More and more stars were flickering through the thinning clouds.

"Yes," she said. "I know. The final humiliation. . . . You think I don't remember? How many times at the camp didn't I think: Ah, curse Him. Curse Him. Curse Him and have done with it. Still . . ." She pressed her palms together. "Still, one must live."

He nodded and, in order to calm himself, tried to

identify the few constellations that he knew: the Milky Way, the Big Dipper—in Hebrew, the Great Wagon—that was just visible in the north.

"What is it?" Esther asked him. "What's the matter?"

He was weeping. With one hand, he gestured toward the sky. All the clouds had gone, and all motion had ceased. In its place, from horizon to horizon, countless stars were shining, arranged in a vast, quiescent and eternal order that Esther had blessed, and from which he was excluded by the tumult in his rebellious heart.

The Well

SUNDAY. It's ten-year-old Micah, Aviva's kid, waiting in front of the dining hall just before lunch, who brings us the news: one of the Bedouin camels from Ahmed's camp two kilometers south of the *kibbutz* has strayed into our date grove to give birth. "Come and thee! Come and thee!" he cries. Buck-toothed, and with ugly brick-red hair like his mother, he speaks with a lisp, spraying a fine mist of spit into the air that gives me the fantastic notion that he has somehow boiled over from the heat. ". . . Juth for a minute," he insists. Grossman the mechanic is with me, pale and drawn from his morning's work in the machine shop and his attack of *shil-shul*, the chronic dysentery from which he has suffered the last two days. "Pleath," the boy pleads, but bathed in sweat, and absentmindedly chewing on the ragged end of his drooping mustache, Grossman refuses with a shake of his head, and goes inside, slamming the screen door behind him and stirring up the flies. The boy takes hold of my hand.

"It'll only take a minute."

"Where's your mother?"

A hubbub around us, as more and more of the *chaverim*—the comrades, members of the collective settlement—arrive at the dining hall from the workshops and the fields. They are in much the same state as Grossman and myself, and do not care who knows it: sullen, completely exhausted by the heat, and oppressed by the prospect of a meager meal and an afternoon's work still to be done.

"Oh pleath, pleath," the boy begs, with the rising inflection," the sad whine of the ugly child who has already learned that he cannot command attention any other way. "You don't underthtand."

"Maybe after lunch."

"But that'll be too late. He'th going to kill it."

"Kill what? Who?"

"Oh, hurry!"

It's too much of an effort for me to argue or try and understand, and he knows it. Hand in mine, he leads me away, past the deserted machine shop and the cowshed where, attracted by the feed, literally hundreds of twittering sparrows are perched on the corrugated tin roof—the only life, it seems, besides ourselves, abroad on the desert at this hour of the day.

Just noon. At the date grove, row on row of the broad dusty leaves cast no shadow, offer no refuge from the terrific glare of the sun.

"Look!" says the boy.

"Where?"

I shield my eyes with my hand, and there, in the direction that he points, just beyond the line of trees to the south, is a camel with her colt that couldn't have been born more than an hour before. Beside them, on the ground and swarming with flies, is the bloody sack. A wonderful sight, I must admit. The colt, waist high, as yet with only a rudimentary hump, all knees and huge splayed toes, jerks its head convulsively as it sucks at the pendulous swollen udders of the mare.

"Promith me!"

"What?"

"You won't let him kill it, will you?"

"Who, Micah, what are you talking about?"

This time, he only has to turn his head. To my left, not ten feet away, and apparently watching us all the while, is a young Bedouin with a rifle, squatting on his hams against one of the trees.

"*Shalom.*"

"And peace; peace unto you," he replies, speaking Hebrew with a thick Arabic accent. Under the *kaffiah* that shadows his eyes is a rather handsome, intelligent face; high cheekbones, a hooked nose, and a thick black mustache that droops down to the corners of his mouth.

"Ask him yourself. He says he'th going to kill it. Why?" says the boy, and the Bedouin, for an answer, glances up to indicate—what? In the torpor engendered by the heat, it takes me a moment to fully understand. I too, as though compelled, look up at the cloudless sky from which the sun has bleached all the color, leaving a white, translucent haze that dazzles the eyes.

"Tell me why!"

It's the drought, of course. I try and explain to the boy. Now the middle of November, what little autumnal rains the Bedouin depend on to water their herds is more than six weeks overdue.

"But what about their well?"

"Ah, now that's just the trouble. Their well has all gone dry. The colt has to be killed so that their children will have the milk to drink. You wouldn't want the children to die of thirst, would you?"

"I don't care."

"Micah!"

"Is our well dry too?"

"Not yet; no."

"Why not?"

"It's deeper."

While we have been talking, the Bedouin has opened the bolt of his rifle—an old Lee Enfield .303—and inserted a cartridge with a click that rivets our attention to the oiled barrel gleaming in the sun. When he stands up in his soiled, billowing pantaloons, the boy cannot suppress a shout that makes the mare swivel her head in our direction. She apparently has just become aware of us, and, with a kind of comical, bewildered ferocity, lets hang her protruding underlip, and bares her teeth. The startled colt has stopped sucking, and skitters backwards, with its shaky forelegs locked together, and the back spread awkwardly apart. For the first time, I catch a glimpse of its bitten cord, already withering from its belly like a dead vine.

"*Chaver!* . . . But, comrade!" the boy shouts.

"Micah, come here. Come away."

"Comrade, don't!"

"Come away, I tell you. It's none of our business."

"You promithed!"

"No. There's nothing I can do."

I catch him by the hand and drag him away. At the cowshed, the echoing crack of the shot rouses the sparrows who rise in a dark, twittering mass, circle the silo twice, and begin once again to settle on the sloping tin roof.

Grossman is still in the dining hall when I get back, sitting alone at a corner table.

"Where's the kid?" he asks.

"I left him at the nursery."

"Aviva was looking for him."

"I know. I saw her. How's the stomach?"

"O. K."

"Really better?"

Obviously forcing himself to keep up his strength,

he is eating a plate of white goat's cheese and chopped cucumbers, washing down mouthfuls of the stuff with sips from a cup of cold water.

"The water'll give you cramps."

"No," he says, "I really feel better. . . . So the Bedouin are beginning to slaughter their herds."

"You heard the shot. . . . The kid was terribly upset."

"It's a shame."

"I read in yesterday's paper that the government says if the drought keeps up, they'll try and relocate the tribes to better grazing land up north."

"The government." He grimaces. A stomach spasm? It's hard to tell. With a sour expression on his face, wiping off his mustache, he pushes away the plate of food. "Who is doing the shooting?"

"One of the younger men. Good-looking. He speaks a little Hebrew, I think."

"Don't tell me. Not Ali?"

"Which one is Ali? . . . Oh." I remember Ali, Sheik Ahmed's oldest son, with whom Grossman had struck up a friendship two years before, when, for a season, both of them were shepherds, pasturing their herds together some thirty kilometers or so north of here.

He goes on, "It's a damn shame. By the time the government decides to do anything for them, it'll be too late."

"Not necessarily."

"You know it as well as I do. What's the use? By the time it goes through all the official channels to provide relief, they'll have slaughtered all their young animals. What'll they do come Spring?"

"They'll manage."

"They'll starve. That's what."

Then absorbed in thought, he is silent. All around us, like insects in amber, each sound in the room seems embedded and preserved in the thick air, yellowed by the sunlight streaming through the windows; the clatter of tin forks, scrape of plates, murmur of the comrades' voices, and, pervading all else, the buzz of the flies that are so fat and lazy when they alight you can squash them with a finger.

"Ali, eh?" he asks. "I haven't seen him in over a year. What do you think? Maybe I ought to go over and have a talk with him."

"What you ought to do is go back to your room and lie down."

He gives me an ironic glance and is partly right. It's not his health alone that concerns me, but a reluctance, as elected secretary, more or less a kind of first among equals, general manager of the settlement, to allow the *kibbutz* to become officially involved in Bedouin affairs at all.

"No," I tell him.

"Why not? We were friends."

"You asked my advice and I'm telling you. If they really would like us to help them, let them take the initiative for once—just for once—and come to us."

"I can't see any harm in just talking to Ali."

But there is. That's the trouble, and Grossman knows it as well as I, in spite of any personal relationship he may have cultivated with the Sheik's son. For eleven years now, since the establishment of our settlement in the desert by force of arms, we have lived in a state of truce with Ahmed's tribe, no more and no less. Time and time again, experience has taught us that when we so much as offer them any material assistance, much less demonstrate a willingness for a real peace, it is refused, and taken for nothing but a display of weakness on our part, a loss of face as far as we are concerned.

"No," I continue, "I . . ." But Grossman interrupts by standing up.

"No matter. It was just a thought."

He leaves, but all afternoon in the secretary's office—a desk, two rattan chairs and a metal filing cabinet—I can think of nothing else while I should be at work checking a list of supplies to be bought tomorrow in Beersheva.

". . . twelve kilos baking soda, 10 salt . . ."

Impossible to keep my mind on it. The office, adjacent to the radio shack, stands on a little rise behind the dining hall, commanding a view of the desert to the south. Broken up by a network of wadies running east to west—dry water courses eroded by flash floods—the landscape always gives me the impression that it has been raked by the talons of some gigantic beast. Here and there, glaring in the sun, are white outcroppings of rock—ribs and spines and shoulder blades, with no effort of the imagination at all, only partly buried by the cracked earth. Yes. It is exactly as though some unimaginable animal has dug at the earth to bury the bones of its prey.

" . . . salt, 15 kilos sugar, tea . . ."

Again and again my gaze returns to the window, but at this distance the black wool tents of the Bedouin encampment are indistinguishable among the chaotic pattern of the shadow cast by the afternoon sun on the broken ground. Once, and only for a moment, one of their camels is to be seen, silhouetted against the sky, and again—or is it my imagination?—I can hear the faint echo of a rifle shot borne on the rising wind. Four-thirty. Finished by now with his work at the machine shop, Grossman is there, I am sure of it, but to speak with Ali means nothing. That's the whole point. It is Ahmed himself who has always been responsible for most of the difficulties that exist between us. The absolute ruler of the tribe for over twenty years, he is terrified—and with some justification—that even the minimal communication between the two communities will undermine his feudal authority. I have seen him only once or twice, at the Kassit, or Morris' cafés in Beersheva: a great hulk of a man, not without dignity, who wears a pointed little beard, and whose dark, unhealthy-looking skin reminds me, for some reason, of the color of a slice of apple left exposed to the air. Purportedly still possessed of a harem of twenty women or more, his licentiousness is legendary. One story has it that one day, long ago, at the height of his powers, he came upon a beautiful fourteen-year-old Bedouin girl drawing water from a desert well, and unable to resist making overtures—pleading, threatening, promising her anything to get her to join his harem—he reduced the child to tears.

"Let me go," she begged. "If you don't let me go, I'll tell my father."

"And just who is that?" Ahmed wanted to know.

"A Sheik. A very powerful Sheik who'll have you gelded like a horse."

"Who?" he laughed.

"Ahmed. Do you realize that? Sheik Ahmed," was the reply.

Five-fifteen. Sure enough, Grossman shows up at the office, looking even worse than before, completely drained, with livid lips and feverish eyes.

"So you went."

"Yes. . . ." We walk back to his room and he talks. "Things are terrible there, worse than I imagined. . . . Their well has been dry since the day before yesterday. What water they have will only last them to the end of the week, if they're lucky. They've made up their minds to slaughter most of their herds by then, sell the meat for what they can get in Beersheva, and maybe buy enough water to last them until the rains come. . . ."

"Did you speak to Ali?"

"I was right. It was he that you saw. . . . He agrees with me absolutely. If and when the government acts to help them, it'll be too late."

The evening breeze has already begun blowing from the southwest, drying the sweat from our bodies with a chill, and whipping the sand across the ground with a rasping noise that sets the teeth on edge. We pause in front of the row of attached wooden shacks that serve as the bachelor quarters of the settlement.

"So Ali really was willing to speak with you. . . ."

"Of course. One must be willing simply to—make the effort."

"And Ahmed?"

Grossman laughs. "The old dog. . . . Would you believe it? Ali told me he's developed a taste for European women in his old age. He's actually gone so far as to place advertisements in three or four papers on the Continent for a new concubine—preferably young, fat and blonde.

"But you didn't speak with him?"

"It wasn't necessary."

"He refused to see you?"

"Yes, but it doesn't make any difference. He'll soon be dead. Ali will be Sheik. He has most of the authority right now. . . . I tell you, this is something new. Times have changed."

"I see. And just what did Ali propose?"

"Nothing. He just told me what was happening. Of course, I could see it all with my own eyes. They're desperate. He . . . No. He didn't propose anything."

"But you did."

"No. . . . That is, I suggested. . . . Actually, I wanted to speak with you first."

We go inside his room that resembles nothing so much as a cell with its iron cot and tiled floor. Grossman insists on making coffee, squatting on his hams in front of the kerosene burner in the same posture as Ali against the date palm. Interesting, the similarities between them. It is never so apparent to me as now. Both of them, Arab and Jew, born in the country, reared here, feeling completely a part of it, even resemble each other physically, affecting the same drooping mustache that is probably Turkish in origin, signifying virility. The water begins to boil on the blue flame.

"Yes," repeats Grossman. "You'll see for yourself. Times have changed. . . ."

Does he really believe it? I don't know. Maybe it's so. In any case, what I, as a European immigrant, can never fully comprehend, is the significance of that mustache or peculiar crouch; the sense of utterly belonging in this country of his birth. Whatever the truth concerning the Bedouins may be, it is that which is at the heart of Grossman's passionate desire to affect a rapprochement with the tribe. Knowing no other home, he appreciates and respects the Arab's sense of possession for a land that he loves as well. More—actually speaking fluent Arabic from his childhood, he can remember a time in the not-too-distant past when the two populations lived side by side with no more than the usual conflicts that divide one man from another. The fact that he has fought them, has in fact, within my earliest memory of arriving here, fought bravely against Ahmed himself, who attacked the settlement on the first night of its establishment, seems to him essentially beside the point. Being young, it is the present that counts for him—this moment alone, and the future, when the development of the land that he loves will depend first and foremost on peace.

"Sugar?"

"No thanks."

He hands me a cup, and sits on the cot.

"You realize this is the chance we've been waiting for."

"Maybe."

"But I told you," he says, "Ali will soon be Sheik. If we can just establish good relations with him now . . ."

"But it isn't as if we haven't tried before. What about the drought four years ago? It was the same thing. They refused any help, and then—when was it? You remember. That little girl with appendicitis." He remembers, nodding his head sadly in the diminishing light. Two summers ago, rather than trust us to take one of their children into Beersheva for an operation, they apparently preferred to see her die.

"Still, this is different," he insists. "Ali is different than the old man. He spent almost a year in Tel Aviv, did you know that? Working at the port. With Jews. That's where he learned to speak some Hebrew. For the first time, they're more than willing to accept our help."

"What exactly do you suggest?"

"What about our own well?"

"All right, so far as I understand."

"That's what I thought. We've probably more than enough water to see us all through."

"That I couldn't say."

"Well, enough for at least a week, if we're careful. The rains will be here by then."

"Then what you want is to have us share our water."

"Exactly."

"That's, of course, a decision that neither of us can make alone."

"I realize that," he tells me. "The whole *kibbutz*

will have to decide. That's why I wanted to speak with you. We'll hold a meeting."

"When?"

"You should have seen the camp. . . . They're rationing what water they have, and the kids have sores on their lips—the corners of their mouths. . . . They surrounded me with tin cans, begging for water, as one would beg for alms."

He has neglected to light a lamp. In the gathering dark, his face is almost invisible, and his momentary anguish is communicated only by the timbre of his voice.

"When do you want me to call a meeting?"

"What? . . . Right away. The sooner the better. Tonight, if you can. Right after supper."

"I'll see what I can do."

"Wonderful. Oh. I almost forgot. Tell the night watch to let Ali through, will you?"

"You asked him to come here tonight?"

Under his mustache, his teeth gleam faintly as he grimaces with a stomach pang or smiles to himself in the dark.

"Yes," he tells me. "Of course, about ten."

The meeting, held in the dining hall, attended by about sixty adult members of the settlement, is over by nine forty-five. Simple majority rules, and Grossman's motion is carried by almost two to one after Lev, the engineer who dug our artesian well four years ago, assures us that in all probability there will be enough water to supply the two communities for at least the next week if we are careful. It's agreed that the Bedouin are to be permitted to take as much as they need every morning without charge—on one condition imposed by Zvika, who holds forth from his bench for more than five minutes, his round face shining with sweat, and his eyes bloodshot from the cigarette smoke that hangs in the air. He is a tractor driver, a man of about twenty-eight, prematurely completely bald, and intensely self-conscious about it, so that even indoors his head is always covered by an army fatigue cap, with its peak turned up. A particularly doctrinaire and pedantic Socialist, and an author to boot, he has recently published a book comparing the life of the modern *kibbutz* to the ancient Hebrew Essene and early Christian communes. His high-pitched voice drones on. Now, to illustrate some point he is making, he is actually quoting by heart from Philo, describing the life of the Essenic communes near the Dead Sea that were so much like our own.

"'. . . For none of them wishes to have any property of his own, but rather by joining together everything without exception, they all have a common profit from it. . . .'"

Grossman, glancing at his wristwatch, interrupts him impatiently.

"Philo! Who's Philo? What's this Philo got to do with it?"

"I'm discussing the principles upon which this *kibbutz* has been founded. Principles which . . ."

"But there's a motion on the floor. What's all this have to do with sharing the water with the Bedouin?"

"That's it. Aha! Exactly. Sharing. . . . You are evidently proposing an equitable distribution of the water. All well and good, and in accordance with our principles. But we are dealing here with a feudal lord—a Sheik, don't forget that. What's there to guarantee that Ahmed will distribute our water fairly among his own people? How can we be absolutely sure, for example, that it's not his harem alone, or his relations—who knows? Who are going to benefit? Do I have to tell you . . ."

"I've already explained," says Grossman. "Ali . . ."

"What do I care about Ali? Ahmed, Ahmed is still Sheik and, whether you remember it or not, it was Ahmed who . . ." His shrill voice breaks off, but the rest of the sentence hangs over us as tangibly as the blue smoke. It was Ahmed who ordered the surprise attack on the settlement eleven years ago, and who was responsible for the murder and mutilation of Zvika's first wife, a girl of seventeen. "As a matter of fact," he resumes. . . .

"I guarantee it," says Grossman.

"How?"

"You have my word. I guarantee a fair distribution of the water. I'll supervise myself."

Zvika shrugs. Aviva rises, yawning behind her hand, and suggests that such a guarantee be amended to the original motion. She is exhausted from working all day in the communal laundry, and wants only to be able to go to bed.

"Well?"

A show of hands, throwing a forest of shadows resembling pruned trees against the wall. The amended motion is carried unanimously, and we adjourn.

"Congratulations," I tell Grossman.

"Thanks. Yes. It's a beginning, at least. A step in the right direction."

Outside, the wind is blowing from a blue-black sky that is ablaze with the innumerable stars of the desert night. Grossman shivers as we walk back to his room. The cold is intense. It is as if the sun today had burned away the atmosphere of the earth, exposing us to a chill from outer space itself.

"Ali ought to be here by now. Would you like to come in for a cup of coffee?"

"No thanks. I'm tired. Bed for me."

A little later, while brushing my teeth at the pump that stands outside the row of shacks, I catch a glimpse of them both through the window of Grossman's room. They are standing in the corner, by the orange crate that serves as a bookcase, talking together with cups of coffee in their hands. Once again, their physical resemblance is striking. They are even the same height and, but for the slightly darker cast of the Bedouin's skin, might be taken for blood relatives, cousins, or even brothers, perhaps, with their high cheekbones, and long mustaches that emphasize their thin lips. Are they speaking Arabic or Hebrew? I am too far away to tell. The Bedouin suddenly laughs, touching Grossman on the upper arm. It is not hard to imagine that they are recalling the memories they have of shepherding together, near Halutza. Now Grossman is laughing too, holding his nose. I was right. They are talking about shepherding—the stench of the long-haired sheep, the lonely hours spent under the shade of the cypress tree, with the shared, stale loaf of bread on the grass between them, and the goatskin water bag passed from hand to hand.

Monday, just after dawn, it begins. For almost four hours now, patiently queued in the blazing sun, a long line of Bedouin women—perhaps a hundred of them or more—dressed entirely in flowing robes of black wool, with only their eyes showing, and strings of Turkish coins sewn onto their veils, draw water from the spigot outside of the cowshed. There is no sound but the twittering of the sparrows and the tinkle of coins as, one by one, they bend down and fill the tin cans they have brought with them. The silence is uncanny. Occasionally, on their arms, a naked infant, covered with flies, is to be seen, but it too, as though enjoined by some mysterious command, makes no noise, but only gazes about with solemn, feverish eyes. Grossman and I are supervising. Just from the look of him, he feels no better, worse perhaps, than last night. The exhilaration of getting his motion passed and making arrangements with Ali has worn off. Periodically, he must excuse himself to go to the latrine, and when he returns with an embarrassed smile on his ravaged face, I plead with him to go back to his room and lie down.

"No, no, it's all right. I promised. . . ."

He dozes a little, stretched out in the shadow cast by the overhanging roof, while the black-robed women shuffle by. In the shed, a cow lows. I, too, begin to fall asleep, only to be abruptly awakened by a confused babble of voices, and a piercing shriek.

"What is it? What's happened?" Grossman rubs his eyes.

At the spigot, two of the women have gotten into a row. For some reason, one of them, holding up the line, evidently cannot make up her mind to fill up her rusty can or not. With her hands at her sides, clenching and unclenching one fist, she stares at the stream of water that splashes over the hem of her robe and bare feet, while now four or five of the others flap their arms and rage about her. Then, with another shriek, she is shoved aside, stumbling against Grossman who has come up to them, shouting in Arabic at the top of his voice. Silence again, sudden and complete, broken only by the wail of an infant from somewhere in the crowd.

"What's the trouble?" I ask.

"Turn off the water. . . . Just a minute," he tells me, and then, in Arabic, speaks to the woman who has been thrown against him. In a huddle on the ground, apparently mortified by her physical contact with a strange man, she buries her veiled face in her hands and emits nothing but a high-pitched, quavering wail. It is more than a minute before he can get her to answer. Then, listening attentively, with a puzzled expression on his face, he turns to me.

"I don't understand."

"What does she say?"

"It just doesn't make sense. . . . She says that she and her husband are very poor. They will starve because they own only two milch goats that will die of thirst unless they can get water."

"Then why doesn't she take it?"

"That's what's so confusing. She says she can't afford it."

"Are you sure?"

"Positive."

"But tell her it's free. She can take as much as she needs without charge. Didn't you explain that to Ali?"

"Of course."

"Well, didn't he tell them?"

Again, Grossman questions her, but this time she refuses to answer altogether. It is impossible to determine her age, or even the shape of her body underneath that robe. Only her eyes are visible, yellowed and contracted in the glare of sun.

"Useless. . . ." Grossman straightens up. The other women have fallen back in a silent semi-circle around us. "I just don't get it. There's obviously been a misunderstanding of some kind."

"What are you going to do?"

"I don't know. Ask Ali, I guess."

"Now?"

"I suppose so."

"Wait here, I'll bring the Jeep and go with you."

"No, no, there's no need."

"Do as I say. You're in no condition to drive."

With one hand to his head, he closes his eyes and makes a gesture as if to shake off the weakness that has hold of him.

"I don't know," he says. "Maybe we ought to wait."

"For what?"

"They really can't afford it."

"Afford what? What are you talking about?"

"If we drive over to the camp now, we'll be considered guests. You know their laws of hospitality. They'll feel obliged to slaughter a sheep for a meal."

"You wait here."

The communal Jeep is kept in the machine shop, but it takes me over twenty minutes to locate Chaim who has charge of the keys. He is working in the shack that houses our electric generator, repairing a worn fan belt. I could have spared myself the effort. By the time I drive back to the cowshed, Ali is there. He had apparently just ridden over from the encampment on a small white mare that one of the women holds by the bridle as he dismounts and shakes hands with Grossman who begins talking to him at once, in a low, anxious voice. They are speaking in Hebrew as I come up, each with his forehead almost touching that of the other, and their hands clasped behind them.

"Then you did tell them," Grossman is saying. The Bedouin nods.

"But I still don't understand. If they know we are not charging them anything, why does the woman say she can't afford it?"

"It's nothing."

"There must be a reason."

"She's talking about the tax."

"What tax?"

"A half a pound."

"For what? Whose?"

"My father's. For the use of the water."

Ali is smiling. He is having difficulty in speaking Hebrew so quickly. Now, very slowly, searching for each word— "You mustn't bother yourself."

"Do you mean to tell me that your father is taxing them a half a pound per person for the use of water from our well?"

"But of course."

Grossman is silent. Behind us, an infant gives a stifled cry, and the mare tosses her head and chomps at her bit.

"Let me get this straight . . ."

"But I have already explained," says Ali. "There's no need to concern yourself. This is—" He completes the sentence in Arabic: "—our affair entirely."

"Yes, that's it. It's the law. The tribe must always pay the Sheik for the right to draw water from the well."

"But the water is ours."

The Bedouin gives a barely perceptible shrug.

"Don't you understand?" says Grossman. "It's impossible. I gave my word. . . . The whole point is for us to share with all of your people fairly. . . . An equal distribution."

Again, the Bedouin apparently cannot get the drift of the Hebrew. Grossman must translate.

"Equal?"

"Yes," says Grossman. "That woman, for example. What about those who can't afford it?"

"Equal?" the Bedouin repeats, and then, giving up, he lapses entirely into Arabic.

"What's he say?" I ask Grossman.

"He says it's the law. It's always been the law. He says it's the lord's—his father's—right as Sheik to tax them, just as it was his father's before him, and before that, long before. . . ."

"Before what?"

"He didn't say."

I glance at the Bedouin who is looking beyond me, beyond the sloping tin roof of the cowshed and the date grove, toward the desert where the shadows are diminishing as the sun slowly ascends toward noon. . . . Before. Before us, is of course what he means; long before our possession of the land, our settlement and government, when free, or at least subject only to his own law, the Bedouin roamed the desert that belonged to him alone.

"No," says Grossman. "It's out of the question. At the meeting, I promised . . ." and then, in a final effort to make himself understood, he too continues in Arabic. Before he has finished, the sun has reached its zenith. His eyes are glazed, his face streaked with sweat. The Bedouin says nothing until, with a hopeless gesture, one palm upraised, he abruptly turns on his naked heel and walks with dignity toward the waiting mare. The little horse takes a mincing step as he swings himself into the wooden saddle and shouts a word of command to the waiting women, one of whom catches his reins as he leads them away. For almost a minute after they are out of sight, their dust hangs in the air. Grossman coughs, and with averted eyes, and saying nothing, goes down on one knee to the spigot, where he catches a few drops of water that cling to the spout, and moistens his parched lips.

Tuesday and Wednesday. Not a cloud. No sign of rain. The colorless sky is empty but for the flocks of ravens that wheel in gigantic circles above the Bedouin camp. From morning to night they are to be seen like spots before the eyes, the symptom of some madness induced by the heat of the sun. Now there can be no doubt of it; without water, the Bedouin are slaughtering the remainder of their herds to be sold as meat in the market on Thursday in Beersheva. Although I am sure he is aware of what is happening, Grossman makes no mention of it. All day Tuesday he is too sick even to get out of bed. Some of the women take turns bringing him tea and toast, and emptying his bedpan, and for the rest of the time he lies perfectly still, with his face to the wall. Then, as is sometimes the case, on Thursday morning, although greatly weakened, his stomach spasms have subsided sufficiently for him to get up. Restless and inordinately thirsty, he haunts my office where I am busy writing a letter to Tnuva, the cooperative marketing organization of the *kibbutzim* that is negotiating with us for the export of our dates overseas. For what seems to be an hour, he sits by the window facing south, sucking on an orange and brushing away the flies that settle on his face and arms.

"What do you think?" he asks at last. "I suppose it's really Ahmed's fault."

I put down my pen. "I guess so."

"Still, it's a shame. There must be something that can be done."

Then, for a while longer, he is silent. Again a ray of sunlight, riddled with dust, illuminates his face. In the past few days he has lost weight and looks somehow five years younger and more vulnerable than he really is—twenty-six or -seven at the most. The drooping mustache seems more of an affectation than ever, a pretense of manhood pasted on by a kid.

"I don't suppose Ali was here while I was sick."

"No."

"No, I didn't think so. He'll never come back now. . . . Strange. How well it was going that night when he and I had coffee in my room. Ai, if you only knew how sick of it all I am!"

"Of what?"

"This—hatred. Did you know that eleven years ago, the night of the attack, I was the one who found Chava?"

Chava?"

"You remember. Zvika's wife."

"Chava. Yes."

"She was sleeping in her tent when they came. They went at her with their knives when she was still alive. I've never told Zvika, of course, but she was still alive when I found her. Sometimes, you know, I still—have dreams."

"But you don't hate them."

"The Bedouin? I did. Oh, how I did. It's just—how can I possibly explain it? I told you. It makes me sick. All these years, one thing bringing another—endless."

More silence. He rises abruptly from his chair.

"Who can say? I wonder if it'll do any good now."

"What's that?" I ask.

"It couldn't do any harm."

"What?"

"It might still help. You never know."

"I see. You want to go to their camp and try to speak with Ali again."

"Yes."

Now it is my turn to say nothing. He shreds the pulp from the orange rind with his teeth.

"It'll be unofficial, of course. No one here will ever know, except you and me."

"Then why tell me?"

"Because I thought you understood. Don't you see? It's better than not doing anything—letting it go on and on. What is there to lose?"

"I don't know."

"Nothing, I tell you. Come with me," he says. "You'll see."

I screw on the top of the fountain pen. My sweating wrist has smudged the ink on the letter. It will have to be done over again. "If that's what you really want."

"Yes."

We take the Jeep. South of the settlement, there is only a narrow dirt track that eventually leads to the Egyptian border, just north of Nitzana. Surrounded by the white rocks, we are in the valley of the bones, but even here, in the mouths of the wadies, there is still some scrub vegetation left alive, a gray-green stubble encrusted by the white shells of countless snails. Not a tree is to be seen.

"How far now?"

"A half a kilometer. Less," Grossman shouts. Ahead of us, and to the left, where the track intersects with still another narrower path that leads between the rocks, he slows down.

"Their well."

It takes me a moment to be able to distinguish the ruin as a ring of man-raised stones, about knee high, and plastered together with sun-baked mud. He shrugs and drives on, now off the track itself, and up the floor of a huge wadi that runs parallel to the patch among the rocks. When he stops, only one black tent can be seen to our right. The rest are apparently hidden around the bend of the wadi walls that are over ten feet tall.

"Where is everybody?"

"Hiding," Grossman explains.

"Are they afraid?"

"It's just the way they are with strangers."

"Well, there's Ali, at any rate."

"Where?"

He is standing with another man in the shadow of a huge boulder about fifty yards away, near the half-skinned carcasses of four or five freshly slaughtered sheep that lie on the ground covered by a cloud of flies. The blood and flies, the cry of the ravens whose shadows flit across the ground—even the untended fire of dried camel dung smoking in front of the tent—give the impression that some kind of sudden catastrophe has overwhelmed the camp. The naked child completes the picture. A little boy, perhaps six years old, with a swollen belly and shaven skull, emerges from the tent at our approach with a tin can in his hands. BRANDIED APRICOTS, printed in English, coming from God knows where, part of the label is clearly visible as he thrusts it before us, begging for water without a sound.

"Give him your canteen," whispers Grossman, "and wait here."

He starts forward. The child, for some reason, refuses to drink from the canteen itself. I must pour the water into the rusty can, but there is too much of it, and it spills to the ground.

"Wait!" I cry, but it is too late. He has already turned and disappeared once more into the tent. Now Grossman is talking, rapidly, and in an undertone, to

Ali, in Arabic, standing with the bloody carcass of the sheep on the ground between them. The second Bedouin has taken a little step to the left, and for the first time I can see him clearly. It's the old man himself, Ahmed, the Sheik, fatter and older than I remember him, with a fuller beard that has turned completely gray. Still, unmistakably, it is he: carrying himself erect, with his shoulders back, and one hand playing with the hilt of a silver dagger stuck in the yellow sash around his waist. Ali has begun to talk too, for the first time, in a loud, clear voice. The old man glances at him, and, either because the sun is in his eyes, or because something his son has said amuses him, he screws up his face and shows his teeth in a grimace that could be taken for a smile. Behind me, the child, or someone, stirs in the tent, and when again I look around what happens next happens so quickly that it is only later, in retrospect, that I can visualize it all as a piece. Ali is talking, gesturing with his hands, and suddenly, without warning, Grossman has lunged at him, slipping on the bloody ground, so that he is only able to give the Bedouin a glancing blow on the right cheek with his fist. They are down, the both of them, and for the moment, incredulous, neither I nor the old man can make a move. He is still grimacing, the smile frozen on his face, his fingers spread on the hilt of the knife. A moment more, and both of us still remain where we are. Grossman is the first to get to his feet, staring stupidly down at the Bedouin who holds his hand to his cheek and rocks his head slightly from side to side. When I come up, the old man retreats another step to the left.

"What's happened?" I ask.

No answer. "What is it?" Still no response. With his mouth open, and the same stupefied expression on his face, Grossman reaches out his hand with the evident intention of helping Ali to his feet. "Tell me," I repeat. The hand, smeared with sheep's blood, is still extended, but now the Bedouin drags himself back on his elbows and spits on the ground with disgust.

"He blames us for everything," says Grossman, getting behind the wheel of the Jeep. "The fact that they've lost their herds—this morning, a child died—everything. There was nothing I could say. He says his father is right. We've taken their land, and now deny them water."

He tries to turn on the ignition, but fumbles with the keys. His hand is trembling. I glance up. The two Bedouin are standing in front of the tent. Something apparently has struck them as funny. The old man, at least, is laughing deep in his throat, with his head thrown back and his hand still on the hilt of his dagger.

"Why did you hit him?" I ask.

The engine starts with a roar. I have to repeat the question.

"Ah, dog," Grossman replies, looking away. "What else could I do? He called me a dog of a Jew."

THEN AND NOW: AMERICA

The American

HESTER STREET, Number 225. The house where my cousin Shulim and his parents lived has long since been torn down. A furniture warehouse stands in its place. Yet, sometimes, even now, at the age of sixty-five, he will go and gaze at the spot where they rented a three-room cold-water flat in the Winter of 1913, after moving from the Brownsville section of Brooklyn, to try their luck on Manhattan's Lower East Side.

"Actually, it was two rooms and a kitchen," he says. "Freezing, with one toilet out in the hall for the whole third floor. It was a terrible winter. A week after we moved in, the pipes froze. Pfew! What a stink!"

With his hands in his pockets, puffing on a cigar, he'll spend an hour or so strolling up and down the block before he grabs a cab to go home. He's a retired pattern-maker with a pension from the I.L.G.W.U. who lives with his daughter on Madison Avenue and Eighty-fifth Street. She worries about his staying out late, but once in a while he makes an extra stop at Greene Street, where he and his father worked in a dress factory for six dollars apiece a week.

As he describes it, they faced each other across a wide table, sewing sleeves on Singers that dripped oil into wooden dishes they held on their laps. The vibrating needle reverberated in the boy's head. At night, he sometimes dreamed that his numbed fingers slipped and were pierced to the bone.

Saturday, the Jewish Sabbath, was the only day they had off, the only time the boy seemed able to think. In the mornings and evenings, he and his father went to Temple Israel, on Orchard Street, to pray.

Above the Ark was a bronze tablet of the Ten Commandments supported on either side by a gilt lion on its hind legs, half as tall as a man, with a curling tongue and long claws. It seemed to Shulim that the ferocious beasts were scrutinizing the crowd of worshippers for the least transgression against the Holy Law. No matter where you sat in the tiny synagogue those blank eyes seemed to be watching you. Yet the boy believed that if God was just, He was also merciful. If was He who had granted Shulim and his parents a chance to come to America and begin a new life. They had fled Odessa in 1900, after a pogrom. Things were rough in the States, but they were going to get better, the boy was convinced of it. Next year, or the year after that, if all went well, he planned to enter night school and get a high school education. With an education, in America, anything was possible. He could become a clerk or a salesman, or maybe even someday save up enough money to go into some kind of business for himself.

Then, one Saturday, at noon, when the morning service in the synagogue was over, and they were about to go home, his father suddenly gasped and grabbed his arm.

"What is it, Papa? What's the matter?" Shulim asked.

"Nothing. Why?"

"You're as pale as a ghost."

"It's nothing," his father repeated, sitting back down on the bench. The color was beginning to come back to his face, but the expression of stupefied horror in his moist, dark-brown eyes remained the same. What—or whom—had he seen? The boy looked up. Walking up the aisle to his right was a little man with a graying, reddish beard.

"Who's that?" Shulim whispered.

"Where?" his father asked. Straightening up, he folded his prayer shawl and led his son out into the street. The red-bearded man was gone.

"Do you know him?" asked Shulim.

"Who?" said his father. But when they got home, and sat down to dinner, he leaned across the table and announced to his wife in a trembling voice:

"Moscowitz is here."

"Moscowitz?"

"From Hamburg. The boat."

They exchanged glances over their steaming bowls of soup, but refused to say anything more. So that was it, thought Shulim, picking up his spoon. This Moscowitz was someone his parents knew from the ship that had brought them all from Hamburg to New York.

Then what was all the fuss about? the boy wondered. According to what he heard around the neighborhood the following week, Moscowitz was a respectable and charitable widower who lived alone on the next block, supported by his son who had a job as a traveling salesman with a sweater firm uptown. As a matter of fact, it was the old man who had donated the gilt lions for the Ark, in memory of a daughter who had died in Europe on the way to the States. And sure enough, there he was, at the next Saturday's morning service, seated in the place of honor, on the front bench, next to the east wall. His red beard waggled when he prayed. So his son had made good!

Sweating over his sewing machine the next day, Shulim glanced up at his father's bony, yellow face. At the age of fifty, his beard was completely gray. But Moscowitz was retired. How had his son gotten his start? Had he gone to school, or gotten the job with the sweater firm on his own—beginning as a stock boy, perhaps, and working his way up? By now he was probably driving his own car, and making seventy-five or a hundred dollars a week. Shulim tried to imagine what a job like that would be like. It would mean traveling all over the States in his own Ford, or maybe even a Maxwell or Pierce-Arrow. He would wear starched white shirts, a clean one every day, with detachable celluloid collars, and bow ties. At the fancy hotels where he stopped, the bellhops would carry his sample cases. But best of all, his father would be able to quit work. He pictured him reading the Yiddish paper in bed, with his morning glass of tea, and making a donation to the synagogue of new silver bells for the Scrolls of the Law. Bells? Handles, too, made entirely of silver, or a stained glass window inscribed at the bottom with his name. The problem was, how to begin?

The foreman heaped another pile of cotton dresses on the table before him, and he went back to work. By evening, he had it all figured out. Moscowitz's son would get him a job. If the sweater house had hired one boy from Hester Street, then why not another, willing to work just as hard, for the chance to learn the business, and prove his worth?

The boy counted the days until Saturday. The only trouble was that when his father saw Moscowitz in the synagogue, striding up the aisle with his ivory-handled cane, he averted his eyes. "Yes, all right, I knew him," he finally admitted after dinner at home.

"His son too?" asked Shulim.

"Yes, his son too."

"What was he like?"

"It was a long time ago. He was a little boy."

"Was he smart?"

"His father thought so."

"As smart as me?"

"I suppose so. I tell you I can't remember. He was seasick the whole trip. Your mother soaked bread in coffee and tried to feed him, but he couldn't hold it down. Why do you ask?"

"They say he has a very good job."

"Do they?" said his father. A heavy smoker, except today, on the Sabbath, when it was forbidden for a pious Jew to light a fire, he sucked on a wooden match and closed his eyes.

"Do you think the old man would remember you after all these years?" Shulim asked.

"Your father's exhausted. Let him sleep," said his mother, coming in from the kitchen, and sitting down. The boy stared in silence at the plaster peeling from the ceiling above his head. With the rat holes in the woodwork, stuffed with rags, the room had never been as hateful to him as it was now. It was freezing. He could see his own breath when he spoke. Old man Moscowitz lived in Number 321, a building that had hot water and steam heat.

"Why doesn't Papa speak to him?" Shulim asked his mother. "Maybe his son could get me a job."

"Keep your voice down," she told him, a finger to her lips.

The weeks passed. Now whenever he saw Moscowitz in the synagogue—as an additional honor, the old man was invariably called third for the reading of the Law—Shulim was tempted to take matters into his own hands and introduce himself. The rumor was that his son was about to return to New York from an extended selling trip to the Midwest.

"I'll speak to him then," Shulim decided.

But a few days later, when he caught a glimpse of the salesman getting out of his car on Orchard Street, the boy discovered that he had lost his nerve. It was nine o'clock at night. He had just finished work, and he was ashamed of his oil-stained pants and the sweater his mother had patched at the elbows with squares of red cotton snipped from a quilt. He stepped into the doorway of a liquor store to watch. It was Moscowitz's son, all right; there was no mistaking him. Taller than his father, and fatter, with a ruddy face, he had the same greenish eyes and thinning red hair. He even carried the same kind of cane. There was a girl with him, hanging on his arm, who wore a feather boa and a dark-blue coat. The salesman whispered in her ear, and she laughed.

They disappeared around the corner, and Shulim inspected the car. It was a new Maxwell, a shiny black four-seater, with a cone clutch, and red-leather seats. How fast could it go? Unless he missed his guess, it had a 25-horsepower motor at least, or maybe even more. The polished steel fenders reflected the boy's pale, grinning face.

"But why can't you just say hello?" he asked his father as soon as he got home.

"Because he wouldn't remember me."

"His father would."

"Yes, that's possible."

"Then do it for me," said the boy.

"I can't."

"But why not?"

"Because I have nothing to say to him."

"Well, to begin with, you could talk over old times. Hamburg and the boat."

"Impossible."

"Why?"

"Because that's where he left her."

"Who?"

"Moscowitz. The old man."

"No, I mean who did he leave?" asked the boy.

"His daughter."

"I don't understand."

"It's very simple. He had a daughter, but he left her behind in Hamburg because she was sick and they wouldn't let her on the boat."

"How do you know?"

"I was there. Yes, I saw it all. It was the night before we sailed. I was up on the deck having a smoke, and there he was with his son and daughter. She was in his arms, all wrapped up in a woollen blanket, coughing, and spitting up blood. He carried her all the way from Lublin, her father says, but one look and the captain tells him that it's impossible. Against all the health regulations. She would infect the whole ship and, even if she managed to get to America alive, the authorities here would only send her back."

"Is that true?"

"It's the rule."

"What happened then?"

"They called a doctor. A little German with a blond beard and a gold watch who took her pulse. 'Two, maybe three months at the most,' he tells them. 'That is, if she's lucky. Probably less.' 'Three months?' says Moscowitz, opening his purse. Eight or ten Marks are all he has left and, what's worse, he has no German visa. If he stays in Germany for more than a week, they'll send them all back to Lublin where the girl's mother died of the same thing."

"So he left her just like that?"

"The doctor took her to a charity hospital. 'It's all right, Papa,' she says, when they're loading her on the ambulance. 'I'll wear my green dress.' "

"What'd she mean?"

"Who knows? She was out of her mind from the fever. Moscowitz kisses her hand and cries. 'What else could I have done?' he asks me all the way across. 'Go back to Lublin? Do you know what Lublin is like for the Jews? What about my son? Look at him. A strong, healthy boy, absolutely brilliant. Doesn't a boy like that deserve half a chance?' "

The salesman stayed in New York for another week. After work, as exhausted as he was, Shulim found himself roaming the neighborhood looking for the Maxwell. What a car! The advertisements in the newspapers—"The Maxwell: perfectly simple, and simply perfect"—proved him right. It had a 25-horsepower monobloc, side valve engine, and this year, for the first time, it was going to be raced at Indianapolis.

Indianapolis! Would he ever get to see Indianapolis, Des Moines, or Chicago now? He crossed Orchard and Ludlow Streets. America was waiting for him. There were vast open spaces and cities to be conquered out there, a fortune to be made by any young man who was willing to work hard, and who knew his stuff. Essex Street. He had read somewhere that in Chicago there were great hotels with marble columns in the lobby where a traveling salesman could press a button in his room, and be served a steak dinner, on silver plate, by a waiter dressed in a red jacket and boiled shirt. Where had he read about that? He couldn't remember. On Canal Street, an old drunk with white whiskers and a gash on his forehead, clotted with blood, brushed up against him and staggered by, muttering under his breath. In the gutter, a pushcart peddler was seized with a sneezing fit that left him purple in the face. A Jew, obviously. Where was he from? Were his kids going to be pushcart peddlers too? The boy headed home. It was a warmish night, just after a rain. The wet streets were jammed with Jews, Irish and Italians dragging their tired feet, grateful for a breath of fresh air. The toilets in 225 were still clogged. As he walked up the stairs, the boy thought he heard a rat scuttling on the second landing. It was pitch dark. He leaned against the broken banister and held his breath. The hallway stank of excrement and chicken fat. He was suffocating. It was already past midnight. Tomorrow morning was here. He would be up at five as usual to go to work. What for? What was going to happen to him? Had his parents brought him all that way for nothing?

Next Saturday evening, Moscowitz brought his son to synagogue for the final service of the day. Shulim watched them out of the corner of his eye. As far as he could tell, the gilt lions dedicated to the memory of his sister made no impression on the salesman at all. Perhaps he didn't know the truth. Even when his father was called up to read a portion of the Torah aloud, he looked impatient and bored. Once or twice he yawned behind his hand. When the congregation was called upon to stand, he rose with a groan. No, Shulim decided, it was inconceivable that he knew what had happened to his sister. The boy looked at the Ark which had just been closed, and the gilt lions. Old man Moscowitz resumed his seat, and smiled at his son who shook his hand. Did the old fool really think he could bribe the Almighty with a pair of plaster lions covered with gold paint? How old was the girl when she had been deserted? Had she been older or younger than her brother? Older, probably, thought Shulim. He imagined her at fifteen or sixteen with red hair, in that green dress that revealed her developing breasts. She hadn't realized what was being done to her. But how did these things work? Had the fever broken before she had died? Supposing one night she had awakened in that strange hospital, with a perfectly clear head? Would God permit such a thing? He pictured her trying to speak with the blond doctor who had come into the room to take her pulse. It was horrible. Wasn't Moscowitz afraid? America, a hundred dollars a week, and a new Maxwell with red-leather seats for his son. What good would it all do him when God had His revenge? And what about the salesman himself? Would he be punished too? He was yawning again. On Monday, he would be off on another trip.

It was getting dark. The service was almost finished. The rabbi lit the candles in front of the Ark. In the flickering light, the gilt lions seemed almost alive. Their elongated shadows leaped on the east wall. A warning, thought Shulim, as he and his father stood up to leave. The ravening mouths and curved talons were a warning to Moscowitz of the divine justice that was soon to be meted out.

"What can you expect?" says Shulim. "I was just a kid. Actually, the story has a happy ending. The old man lived to be eighty-one, and the last time I heard of the son, in 1924, he was in business for himself, knitwear, and doing very well."

The Law

On and off, that whole summer, I wondered what my uncle Willi was going to do about his son. The boy, Danny, was going to be thirteen on the twelfth of July, and as early as February, I remembered, Willi was talking about having his Bar Mitzvah at their Temple in Queens; the whole works—a service in the morning and a party for the family and their friends in the afternoon at their home.

"Nothing ostentatious, you understand," he told me. "Drinks and hors d'oeuvres. You know: franks, little pigs in a blanket, or lox on pieces of toast."

I said that I thought that the party was a nice idea but, though it was really none of my business, maybe that was enough.

"I mean why the whole service? You don't want to make him go through all of that speechmaking."

"Ah, but he insists," said Willi.

"Does he?"

"So help me. He says he wouldn't think of having one without the other, and his doctor says it's all right.

The doctor says if he really wants to speak, then by all means. Treat him normal."

"What doctor?"

"Rhinehart. Didn't I tell you? Rhinehart's been treating him since the Fall."

"Who's Rhinehart?"

"I thought you knew. Didn't Helene tell you? Speech therapy. One of the big speech men in New York. He's connected with the Medical Center. Just since September, and he's done wonders."

"I didn't know. I'm glad to hear it."

"Will you come to the service?" he asked.

"When will it be?"

"The weekend after the Fourth. That Saturday, in the morning. The Fourth is on a Monday. That Saturday, the ninth," he said.

"Sure."

"Ten o'clock in the morning. Don't you forget now. Mark it down," he said.

I never thought he'd go through with it. For as long as I could remember, his son had a terrible stammer. Just to say "hello" was an effort. He had a habit of closing his eyes as though he'd been told to visualize the word beforehand. It was agonizing to watch: the shut eyes, the deep breath, the pulse beating in his neck, the chin jerking spasmodically, and the spit gathering in the corners of his mouth.

"H-h-h-hello, Joe," he'd greet me. "How-how-how are ya?"

Relaxed, silent, he seemed another kid, somehow altogether different-looking, resembling his mother, with a placid oval face, and large dark eyes, beautiful eyes, with long curly lashes, and delicate hands with bitten nails that were always in his mouth. To avoid speaking as much as possible, he had developed the facility of listening attentively, fixing those eyes on you, with a faint smile on his lips, nodding or shaking his head as the occasion demanded, so that he gave the impression of following whatever you said with a kind of ravenous intensity that made you self-conscious of being able to speak normally yourself. An intelligent defense. That he was really brilliant, there wasn't any doubt.

"An 'A' average in school," Willi told me, throwing his arm about the boy's shoulders. "He loves history," he added, as a kind of concession to me. A pause, as though I was supposed to test the boy's knowledge. Helene, his mother, glanced at me with alarm. I remained silent, smiling with a nod, and it seemed to me that the boy himself gave me a look of gratitude that went unnoticed by his father. At the time, I was teaching American history to the tenth grade in a private school on the Upper East Side. It was easy to imagine Danny's suffering in class, called upon by his teacher to recite, straining to express himself, while the other kids laughed behind their hands, or mimicked him, spraying the air with spit.

Anyhow, that was in February, as I've said. Came the summer and I didn't see much of them at first. I spent most of my time in the Forty-second Street Library doing research for my Ph.D. thesis on the Alien and Sedition Act. A couple of times in May Willi called me on the phone to invite me out to dinner, but I was too busy. He was really the only family I had left, but with one thing and another, we were never really close. My mother's younger brother, a man in his middle forties, short and powerfully built, running now to fat, with red cheeks and a fringe of dark hair about the crown of his head that resembled a monk's tonsure, he always reminded me of the picture of the jolly monk on the labels of imported German beer. He had been born in Germany, as a matter of fact. My mother had written and tried to persuade him to leave the country in 1935, but he intended to study law at Heidelberg, so the Nazis caught him and deported him to Bergen Belsen where he managed to survive the war, coming to this country in 1947, just before my mother's death. He had written a book about his experiences—*Mein Erlebnis*—that was never actually published, but everyone who knew him felt they had read it anyhow, from the way he constantly spoke of what had happened to him. When he spoke about the concentration camps, he sounded as if he was quoting by heart from a manuscript. He generally loved to talk, and if it was a blow to his pride that his son had so much trouble in getting a word out straight, he never let on, as far as I could see.

"Stammering? What's a stammer?" I once heard him tell the boy. "It's a sign of greatness. . . . Yes, I mean it. Demosthenes stammered, and Moses. *Moshe Ribenue*. Mose our Teacher himself."

"M-M-Moses?"

"The luckiest thing that ever happened, believe you me."

"H-h-how l-lucky?"

"How many Commandments are there?"

His son held up his ten fingers.

"Ten! There you are!" said his father. "Believe me, if he didn't have a stammer he would have given us a hundred. . . . Luck, eh? Luck or not?"

The boy laughed. His father had a way with words, there was no doubt of it, making a good living as a paper-box salesman for a company at New Hyde Park on the Island. I imagine he cleared over twenty thousand a year. He lived nicely enough, in one of those red-brick, two-storey, semi-detached houses on Eighty-first Avenue in Queens, with a little rose garden in the back and a pine-paneled bar and rumpus room in the cellar where he intended to have the party after the Bar Mitzvah. I finally went out for dinner the second week in May. We had a drink downstairs.

"You can't help it," he said. "I figure about thirty, thirty-five people. What can I do? Helene's family, friends from the office, the kid's friends from school, the rabbi and his wife. Thirty-five, maybe more. . . . Helene says with that many we'll have to serve lunch. I thought maybe a cold buffet. We'll eat down here. I'm having it air-conditioned."

"It's a nice idea."

"It'll be a nice party, you wait and see. How about another Scotch?"

"Just a drop."

"Chivas Regal. Twenty years old. Like velvet water."

"Just a splash of water," I told him. "Where's Danny?"

"What's the time?"

"Just six."

"Be home any minute. He's at Hebrew school."

"How's he doing?"

"Wonderful. That rabbi does wonders. The boy can already read. Of course, it's all modern. To help him he has a recording of the Haftorah he has to say, put out by some company in New Jersey."

"Sounds like a wonderful idea."

"He's reciting from Numbers."

"I don't know too much about it."

"It's some of the Laws, and how they should organize themselves in the march through the desert."

"And Danny likes it?" I asked.

"You should hear him. The rabbi, the doctor, Rhinehart—I told you: everybody helps. Ask him yourself."

He came home about six-thirty, with his notebook under his arm. He had grown a little since I saw him last, become a little leaner, with bigger hands and feet, bony wrists. There was a slight down on his cheeks and upper lip, but so far as I could tell his speech was about the same. He went through the convulsions just to say hello—the suspended breath and shut eyes, the blue veins swelling on the sides of his neck. When we sat down at the dinner table, he remained standing by his place, with a loaf of bread covered by a linen napkin set before him, and a black silk skull-cap on the back of his head.

"*B-b-b-b-aruch atar a-adonoi,*" he mumbled—the Hebrew blessing of the bread—and when he finished, he looked pale and wiped the spit from his lips with the back of his hand.

"How was that?" Willi asked me.

"Nice."

"Practice. Practice makes perfect."

His son lowered his quivering eyelids. Helene served the roast chicken and wild rice, with little brown potatoes.

"You never learned the language?" Willi spoke to me again.

"I was never Bar Mitzvahed; no."

"Neither was I."

"Really?"

"In Germany, when I was growing up, it was—unfashionable to be given a Jewish education." He tore at a chicken wing with his teeth. "Once in a while in the camp I would run into somebody who could speak Hebrew. It's really an ugly language. It's just that . . . I don't know. It was nice to hear it spoken. It was *verboten,* of course, but still . . . how can I explain? It was something out of our past, the really distant past. It somehow seemed to me to be the only part of our consciousness that was left—uncontaminated. Not like Yiddish. . . . I always hated Yiddish. I used to pride myself on my command of German, the way I wrote particularly, a really educated style, but I learned to hate it. Sometimes for weeks I couldn't bring myself to say a word. The language of the S.S. . . ."

"T-t-t-tell about H-H-Heinz," interrupted his son.

"Eat your chicken," his mother said. The tone of her voice made me look at her with surprise: black hair with a faint reddish tinge, and long curling eyelashes that shadowed her prominent cheekbones. Lucky enough to have been spared the later horrors, she too was a refuge, coming from Germany in 1936. I suddenly sensed that she disapproved and was even a little frightened of Willi's imposition of the whole thing on the boy's consciousness. In front of me, though, "eat your chicken" was all that she said. We finished the rest of the meal in silence—lemon meringue pie and coffee—and Willi, the boy, and myself went into the living room and sat down on the sofa.

"Cigar?" Willi asked.

"No thanks."

He belched and lit up, and began to pick his front teeth with the folded cellophane. "How about a little brandy?"

"That'd be nice."

"Napoleon: the best," he said, pouring some into two snifters that the boy had brought in from the kitchen. "Wonderful. . . . Too good. I'm getting too fat, I know. Soft," he said, patting his paunch. "The doctor tells me I ought to lose at least twenty pounds. An irony, eh? Did you know that when I got out of Belsen I weighed ninety pounds? Ninety, mind you, and now, like all the other Americans, I'm to die of overweight."

His eyes gleamed as though he derived some sort of satisfaction out of the thought.

"A living skeleton," he went on. "You must have seen photos after the liberation of a place like that. I don't have to tell you. . . ."

But he did, as I knew he would; he went on and on, while his son listened, his legs tucked under him, biting on one fingernail after the other.

"You can't know—thank God—not you, or Danny

here, or Helene. . . . No one who was not there can even guess what it was like to be so hungry, to be literally starving to death on two slices of bread a day, and a pint of watery soup with a snip of turnip in it, if you're lucky. Twice a week a spoonful of rancid butter, and an ounce of sausage or cheese. . . . And the worst of it knowing that it's endless, knowing that no matter how hungry you are today there's absolutely no possibility of getting anything more to eat tomorrow but that the anguish will simply grow and grow and grow. . . . Words. . . ." He shrugged. "You aren't really listening and I can't blame you. What good are words to describe such things?"

He sucked on his cigar and screwed up his eyes to watch the smoke, as thick and white as milk, gather in the cone of light above the lamp on the coffee table. "There were two obsessions that everyone had. Ask anyone who was in such a place. Have you ever read any books about them? . . . Food first: dreaming about food, sitting down to a meal like we just had, and eating till you burst, and second: just staying alive so that you would be able to describe what was happening to you. Everyone wanted to write a book. Seriously. Just to tell the world, as though to convince ourselves as well that such things were really happening, that we were actually living through them. I wrote *Mein Erlebnis* in six weeks. . . ."

He waved the smoke away, and again his narrowed eyes had that peculiar gleam. The boy sat perfectly motionless, with his lips slightly parted in expectation of his father to continue, and for the first time I began to understand the nature of Willi's compulsion to talk so much about what he had endured. Triumph. There was a flash of triumph in his eyes as he regarded his son. It was as if I were listening to a mountain climber—what's his name, the one who climbed Everest—or the first man who will land on the moon and live to tell about it. He talked and talked, partly, I am sure, because it was essentially a personal victory that he was describing—and gloating over, in spite of himself. It was a display of prowess before his son; the supreme success, perhaps even the high point of his life, that he among all those millions managed to live through it all.

From the kitchen came the swish of water and the hum of the automatic dishwasher. Helene came into the living room with a bowl of fruit.

"An apple, Joe?"

"No thanks."

Willi peeled a banana, and to be polite perhaps, or maybe because of his wife's feelings about talking as he did in front of the boy, he began to ask me about my work.

"The Alien and Sedition Act, eh?" he said. "Yes. . . . Yes, interesting and significant. . . . When was it again?"

"S-s-seventeen n-ninety-eight," said Danny.

Willi questioned me with a raised eyebrow. "That's right," I told him.

He grinned. "I told you he loves his history."

"He's right a hundred per cent."

"Who was it?" Willi went on. "President Adams, wasn't it? Against the Bill of Rights—the first suspension of habeas corpus."

"And M-M-Marshall," began the boy.

His father laughed with his mouth full of banana. "You can see for yourself he knows much more about it than me." The boy smiled, flushed to his temples with pride. "Still, I remember: No freedom of speech, hundreds of editors thrown into jail for criticizing the government, the prisons packed with dissenters." From his voice, he sounded as though he momentarily somehow enjoyed it.

"About twenty-five, all told," I said.

"You don't say. Just twenty-five?"

"That's it."

He grinned again. "How about that! America, you see?" he said to his wife. "Imagine. A whole stink over that."

"There was more to it than that," I told him.

"Of course, but still—a crisis! Genuine indignation over the fate of just twenty-five men. . . ."

"Yes, partly," I told him, suddenly weary, bleary-eyed from the dinner and the drinks.

"And the Jews?" he asked me.

"I don't understand."

"There was no particular repression of the Jews, as such?"

"I never thought about it, to tell you the truth."

He laughed. "Seriously," I went on. "The law was directed against foreigners, mostly—the British and the French. French spies, for example. There was a lot of spying going on, and the law forced a lot of foreigners to leave the country."

"But nothing was specifically directed against the Jews."

"No. Why should there have been?"

Another laugh. "What's so funny?" I asked him.

"Don't you know the joke?"

"Which one?"

"You must have heard it. . . . The S.S. man in Berlin who grabs a Jew by the collar and kicks him in the shins. 'Tell me, Jew, who's responsible for all of Germany's troubles?' The Jew trembles. His teeth absolutely chatter; his knees knock together. 'The Jews, of course,' he answers. 'Good,' says the S.S. man. 'The Jews and the bareback riders in the circus,' the little Jew goes on. 'Why the bareback riders in the circus?' the S.S. man asks. 'Aha,' comes the answer. 'Exactly! So *nu?* Why the Jews?' "

The boy laughed, slapping his thigh, guffawing until the tears came into his eyes, as if he were delighted to find a release in a sound that he could express without impediment.

"Yes, yes," Willi continued, taking a last bite of the banana and throwing the peel into an ashtray. "He laughs, and it's true, the absurdity, and yet there's something more. There's a reason. . . . Why the Jews? There's the psychology of a Heinz to contend with, and not an isolated pathological case either, but common. More common than you'd care to know."

The boy shifted his position, leaning toward his father with one hand on the arm of the sofa, and both feet on the floor.

"Have a piece of fruit," Helene told me.

"No thanks. Who's Heinz?" I asked.

"Herr Hauptsturmfuehrer Berger," said Willi. "You know the type. Tall and blond, beautiful, really, the very image of manly perfection that you can see for yourself, today, just by going to the movies. . . . A movie star, so help me; six foot two at least, with straight blond hair, white flashing teeth, a positively captivating smile—dimples at the corners of his mouth—beautiful blue eyes. . . . The uniform? Perfection. Designed for him; tailor-made for that slim, hard body, broad shoulders. . . ." He spread his stubby hands in the air, reminding me more than ever of that monk making an invocation. "Black, all black and belted with what do you call them? Riding pants. Jodhpurs, and gleaming black boots. . . ."

"But I still don't understand," I said. "Who is he?"

"*Was,*" corrected Willi. "He was a guard in the camp. After the war the British caught him and he was tried and hanged. . . . *Was.* . . . Unfortunate. I mean it, too. Seriously. No one had the good sense to study him instead: how he used to stand, for example—very significant—with the thumb of one hand, his left hand, I remember, stuck in his belt, and the other grasping a braided riding whip that he would tap against those boots. The boots, the belt, the buckle, the buttons, all flashing in the sun—enough to blind you, believe me. White teeth, that dimpled smile. . . . He was convicted of murder. One day he killed a child, a little girl of seven. . . . In the camp, some of the barracks had three tiers of wooden beds along the wall, bare planks to sleep on, *boxen* in the jargon. We slept together packed like sardines. Often someone would die in the night, but it was impossible to move. We would sleep with the dead, but no matter. . . . Where was I?"

"The child," I said.

"Ah, yes. One of the *boxen* in the women's barracks was coming apart; one leg was coming off. Three tiers, mind you; hundreds of pounds of timber. . . . For some reason the child was on the floor, directly beneath it, on her hands and knees. Perhaps he—Heinz—had ordered it so. I don't know. I don't think so. She must just have been looking for something. A crust of bread, a crumb, perhaps, and in walks the *Hauptsturm-fuehrer* smiling all the while as though to charm the ladies, immediately sizing up the situation; perfect. The child beneath the rickety bed, the girl's mother, Frau Schwarz, in one corner, binding up her swollen legs with a few rags.

" '*Gnädige Frau* . . .' he greets her—the mother, who stands up nervously twisting a rag about her wrist.

" 'Hilda!' she screams. . . . Not even a Jewish name, mind you; a good German name. . . . 'Hilda!' The child begins to rise, but it's too late. With a flick of his boot, a movement of that polished toe, our Heinz has already acted, kicking out the loose timber, bringing down the whole thing on the child's back. . . . A broken back.

" 'Mama!' she cries. 'I can't move! My legs!' For a day and a half like that until she goes into convulsions and dies in her mother's arms. The woman comes to me and reproaches herself because she hasn't got the courage to commit suicide.

" 'After all,' she says, 'I have the means. . . .' She's referring to the rags that she has woven into a noose. 'Just the courage is lacking. Mr. Levy, what's the matter with me?' She goes mad, and before she dies she wanders about the camp asking everyone to strangle her. . . . She even comes to Heinz. It was just outside the latrines. I witnessed this myself. Apparently he doesn't even remember who she is. He shoos her away, those beautiful blue eyes clouded for just an instant in complete bewilderment.

"'*Verrüct*,' he tells me. 'Insane.' With a shrug. I'm busy on my hands and knees scrubbing the concrete floor with a brush and a pail of lye and water, not daring to look up, blinded by those boots.

"'Here, here, Levy. No; to the left. Put some elbow grease into it.'

"A fanatic for order and cleanliness, you understand. He used to speak with me a great deal. I couldn't imagine why. Perhaps because we were both about the same age. He would constantly ask me questions about the Jews—technical questions, so to speak, about our beliefs, about the Torah, for example, all the Laws. He seemed sincerely interested and, as far as I could tell, he was genuinely disappointed when he realized that I knew next to nothing and had been educated like himself as a good, middle-class German—*Gymnasium*, and two semesters at Heidelberg. One day he was absolutely flabbergasted to find out that for the life of me I couldn't even recite the Ten Commandments. I couldn't get more than five, and not in order, either. 'Tsk! Tsk! Levy.' He shook that beautiful head and began reciting them all.

"'I am the Lord thy God who brought thee forth out of the land of Egypt, out of the house of bondage. . . . Thou shalt have no other gods before me.' Etc., etc. All of them, the whole business. . . . Imagine the scene. It was a Sunday, I remember, rest day, the one day off from man-killing labor the whole week. I had gone outside the barracks to get a little sun. Imagine it, I tell you. A vast desert, our own Sinai surrounding us, rolling sand dunes, green wooden shacks set in rows. In the distance, the silver birch trees of the women's camp like a mirage. The wire mesh gate of the main entrance to my right that always reminded me of the entrance to a zoo. Here and there, scattered on the ground, all heaped together, the mounds of bodies, the living dead and the dead—stiff, open eyes, gaping mouths, all heaped together, indistinguishable. It was early Spring, and warm, with a weak sun, gray clouds, cumuli, with a flat base and rounded outlines, piled up like mountains in the western sky. . . . I remember that distinctly—cumuli. . . . It was a matter of life and death, learning to tell one type of cloud from another—the promise of a little rain. There was never enough water. Just two concrete basins to supply the entire camp. We were slowly dying of thirst in addition to everything else. I remember thinking that if the rain does come I shall try and remain outside the barracks as long as I can after roll call, with my mouth open. Crazy thoughts. What was it? Chickens, young *Truthahnen*—turkeys drown that way in the rain, too stupid to close their mouths. . . . Insane, disconnected thoughts while, according to regulation, I stood rigidly at attention, with my chin in, and chest out, my thumbs along the crease in my striped prison pants, as Heinz drones on and on.

"'Honor thy father and thy mother. . . . Thou shalt not murder. . . .' On and on to the end, and then, with what I can only describe as a shy expression on his face, the explanation:

"'We live in Saxony,' he tells me. 'Absolutely charming, Levy. Do you know East Prussia? Ah, the orchard and the flower beds—roses, red and white roses, growing in front of the church. My father's church. A pastor, Levy, and his father before him and before that. Three generations of pastors. When I was young, I thought I would go into the Church myself. I have the religious temperament.'

"'Yes, sir. *Jawohl, Herr Hauptsturmfuehrer.*'

"'Does that astonish you?'

"'Not at all, *Mein Herr.*'

"'It does, of course. . . . Sundays. . . . Ah, a day like today. The church bells echoing in the valley and the peasants in their black suits and creaking shoes shuffling between those rose beds to listen to Papa thunder at them from the pulpit, slamming down his fist. "Love, my friends! It is written that we are to love our neighbors as ourselves." The fist again. "Love!" he shouts, and I would begin to tremble, literally begin to shake. . . . Why, Levy? I often asked myself. You ought to know. Jews are great psychologists. Freud. . . .'

" 'I don't know, *Herr Hauptsturmfuehrer.*'

" 'A pity. . . . He would preach love and all I could see from that front pew was that great fist—the blond hair on the backs of the fingers, the knuckles clenched, white. . . . That huge fist protruding from the black cuff like the hand of God from a thunder cloud. . . .' That was his image, I swear it. So help me, a literary mind. '*Die grosse Faust ist aus der schwarzen Manschette heraus gestreckt wie Gottes-hand aus einer Sturmwolke.* Yet, to be honest,' Heinz went on, 'he never struck me. Not once in my whole life, and I was never what you could call a good child, Levy. Secret vices, a rebellious spirit that had to be broken. . . . And obedience was doubly difficult for the likes of me, but, as I've said, whenever I misbehaved, he never once laid a hand on me. . . . Love. . . . He spoke about love and was silent. Talk about psychology! That silence for days on end; all he had to do was say nothing and I would lie in my bed at night, trembling. Can you explain that, Levy? I would lie awake praying that he would beat me instead, smash me with that fist, flay my back with his belt rather than that love, that silent displeasure. He had thin, pale lips, with a network of wrinkles at the corner of his mouth. . . . No dimples. I get my dimples from my mother. . . . To please him, I would learn whole passages of the Bible by heart; your Bible, Levy.'

"He tapped his whip against the top of his boots.

" 'Tell me, Levy. . . .'

" 'Yes, sir?'

"I know the Jews; a gentle people. Tell me honestly. Did your father ever beat you?'

" 'No, sir.'

" 'Not once?'

" 'Never, sir.'

" 'A gentle people, as I've said, but lax in your education, wouldn't you say?'

" 'Yes, sir.'

" 'Well, then we must remedy that. . . .' "

For the first time, the flow of words faltered. Willi paused to relight his cigar, and then, as though it had left a bad taste in his mouth, snubbed it out in the ashtray and picked a fleck of tobacco from the tip of his tongue. "Like some dog," he finally went on. "As if he were training some animal. . . . That whip across the back, the bridge of the nose, the eyes. . . . All afternoon I stood at attention while those clouds gathered and it began to rain, until I could repeat it all word for word. 'I am the Lord thy God who brought thee forth out of the land of Egypt.' He hit me in the adam's apple. I could hardly speak. The rain came down my face. . . ."

Another silence. The automatic dishwasher had long since stopped. Helene bit into an apple and looked at her watch. Before she had a chance to speak, the boy shook his head.

"Never mind," she told him. "It's late. Past ten. Time for bed."

"Ten?" I repeated, standing up. "I've got to go myself."

"Say good night to Joe," said Helene to her son.

"You w-w-w-wanna hear my r-r-record?" He asked me. "It'll only t-t-take a minute."

"O.K.; for a minute."

His room was at the head of the stairs. I followed him up and he shut the door.

"Y-you never heard about H-H-Heinz before?"

"Never."

"I have; o-often. It used to give me b-bad dreams."

On top of his desk was a phonograph record. He put it on the portable phonograph that stood in one corner of the room. For a time, sitting on the bed while the boy put on his pajamas, I listened to the deep voice chanting in the unintelligible tongue.

"D-don't you understand?"

"Not much," I said.

"How—how come you were never B-B-Bar Mitzvahed?"

"I wasn't as lucky as you. My father was dead, and my mother didn't care one way or the other."

"M-Mama doesn't care either," he said, tying his bathrobe around his waist. He rejected the record and stood by the window that faced the rose garden, biting his thumbnail.

"D-d-do you believe in G-G-God?"

"I don't know."

"I do—do."

"You're lucky there too."

"D-don't you ever pray?"

"No."

"I d-d-do; often."

I imagined that, rather like his laughter, that too must have been a wonderful relief; praying in silence, grateful and convinced that he was able to communicate something without a stammer.

"D-d-do you know what I p-pray for?" he asked me.

"What?"

"A-actually it's a s-s-secret."

"You can tell me if you like."

"S-sometimes, y-you know, when I think of all th-those people at the Temple—at the B-B-Bar Mitzvah, I mean—I get into a sweat."

"It'll be all right."

"There'll be h-hundreds of people there, M-Mama's whole family, G-G-Goldman's parents, and all his family, and all their f-f-friends."

"Who's Goldman?"

"He's a f-f-fink. Sammy Goldman. We're being B-B-Bar Mitzvahed together. He's rich. His father owns a chain of delicatessens. He's t-told everybody about me.

He didn't want to g-go with me. He has p-pimples from p-p-playing with himself."

"It's late," I told him. "I really ought to go."

"It's another m-m-month or so. More. Time enough. Anything can h-h-happen in time, don't you think?"

"It depends."

"If you b-b-believe enough?"

"Maybe so."

"The st-st-stammer, you know, is all psychological. Doctor Rhinehart says so. It c-came all of a sudden. W-when I started school."

"I didn't know."

"Oh yes. And if it c-c-came that way, it can g-g-go too; suddenly, I mean. That's l-l-logical, don't you think?"

"Anything is possible," I told him.

He smiled abruptly, and opened his mouth again, giving me the impression that he wanted to say something more. But for some reason, maybe because he was tired, he got stuck; his chin jerked spasmodically as he tried to force the word from his mouth, and then he shrugged and gave up, holding out a moist palm to say good night and good-by.

"Good luck," I told him.

About a week later his father gave me a ring. He had a customer in the garment district, on Seventh Avenue and Thirty-seventh Street, and he thought that if as usual I was working at the Forty-second Street Library, we could meet for a bite of lunch. I said fine. It was a hot day. His cheeks were purplish from the heat and he breathed heavily. We had a sandwich and a soda at Schrafft's and then he walked me back to the library where we sat for a while on the granite steps under the trees around the flagpole at the north entrance on the avenue. The place was jammed with shopgirls and clerks taking in a few minutes of the sun before they had to go back to work. We sat and watched the flow of crowds going into the stores; the cars and the buses and the cabs, the cop at the intersection, wearing dark glasses and a short-sleeved summer uniform, waving the traffic on.

"How's the work?" Willi asked me.

"Coming along. How's the family?"

"Fine. They send their best."

"Send my love."

"I will." He smoked a cigar and coughed. The air was thick with fumes. "You know, Danny doesn't say much, but he can't fool me."

"About what?"

"He's worried about the Bar Mitzvah. Speaking in front of all those people. I told him to take it slow and everything would be all right. What do you think?"

"You know best."

"Helene thinks I'm doing the wrong thing."

"It's hard for me to say."

"You heard me that night. . . . Sometimes I go on and on. She says I shouldn't fill his head with that sort of thing, but I say that he has a right to know."

"You may be right."

"He doesn't understand everything, of course. . . . That story about Heinz, for example. . . . But he will in time. . . . It was a revelation to me. You know, sometimes, in the camp, before I met Heinz, I used to wonder why it was all happening. Why the Jews, I mean. . . .

"Oh, there are other factors, of course. . . . But don't you see? The Commandments. All the Laws. . . ." He flicked away his cigar ash. "The Law, more than anything. . . . He taught me that, that day in the rain. They were murdering, humiliating us because whether it was true or not we had come to—how shall I say it?—embody, I suppose . . . In some strange way, we had come to embody that very Law that bound them too—through Christianity, I mean—and in destroying us . . . Heinz, for example, hating his father, the pastor, who preached love—love thy neighbor, from Leviticus, you know. . . . Of course, there's the fist: love and hate all mixed together. I really don't understand that part myself, but I do know that what all of them hated, somehow, was the yoke that we had given them so long ago. The Law that makes all the difference, that makes a man different from a beast, the civilized . . ." He coughed. "Can't you see what I mean?"

"I'm not sure. I think so."

"It's hard for me to keep it all straight myself. . . . I just feel that the least we can do is pass it on, the way we always have, from father to son. The Bar Mitzvah. . . . Of course, now with Danny, he doesn't really complain, but he suffers, I know. I'm not sure just what to do."

"What can I tell you?"

"Nothing, I know. I just wanted you to understand. . . . You know the irony is that he hates me."

"Don't be absurd."

"It's true—at least partly. Oh, he loves me too, but Rhinehart says that stammering is very often—it's very complicated—a kind of expression of hostility, resentment, to those whom you're supposed to love. . . . It all started you know when he began school. He was very bright. I've always demanded too damn much of him."

"It'll be O.K."

"Oh, I know it, eventually. It's only that in the meantime . . . I told him yesterday that if he wanted to call the whole service off, I'd be glad to do it in a minute."

"What'd he say?"

"Nothing doing. What he's been saying all along. Definitely not. . . . As a matter of fact, he smiled."

"Did he?" I said. "What are you going to do?"

"Go ahead, I guess. But I made it as clear as I could that any time he wants to drop the speech and just have the party at home, it was more than O.K. by me."

"Well," I told him. "I've got to get back to the books."

"I know. I didn't mean to keep you."

"Thanks for lunch."

"My pleasure. . . . Joe, you're the only blood relative I've got left. People talk. I just wanted you to understand."

I nodded, and left him standing there, smoking and coughing, in the dazzling pattern of light and shadow cast by the sunlight streaming through the dusty leaves of the trees.

The weeks went by. Once or twice he called again to have me out to dinner, and I asked him whether or not the service was still on. "Sure," he'd answer. "He's studying away." I was too busy getting my notes into shape to go out and see them. My work was going fairly well. I decided to attack the whole problem from the point of view of Chief Justice Marshall—the origin of judicial review—but with all of it, I got a good chunk of the reading done by the beginning of July, so that over the Fourth I was able to get away and spend the weekend visiting a classmate of mine at Columbia and his wife who had taken a cottage for the summer at Cape Cod. I got back Tuesday night. The service was scheduled for the following Saturday, so I called Willi to make absolutely sure once and for all that Danny was going to speak in the Temple.

"You bet," he told me. "You know, I think I've got a budding rabbi on my hands."

"How do you mean?"

"Religious? My God, you ought to see him. He gets up at six in the morning to pray."

The service was to be held at Temple Shalom on Seventy-eighth Avenue. I hadn't bought a present yet and I was stumped. For the life of me I couldn't think of anything original. In the end, I went to the bank and bought him a series-E savings bond for $25.00. Somehow it didn't seem enough, so in addition I bought him fourteen silver dollars—one extra for good luck—and had them packed in a velvet box with a clasp. I thought the kid might get a kick out of it.

Saturday at last: hot and muggy, a promise of rain, with a peculiar diffused light shining from behind the low gray clouds. It was too hot to sleep much the night before. I was up at six-thirty and out of the house by a quarter to eight. At first I thought that maybe I'd go out to the house and we'd all go to the Temple together. I don't know why; I decided against it. I loafed around instead, wasting time, and by the time I took the subway and arrived in Queens it was a quarter to ten. The crowds were already arriving at the

Temple, Goldman's relatives, most of them people I didn't know, all dressed up in dark summer suits and light dresses, flowered prints and silks. It was so muggy that the powder flaked on the women's cheeks. I finally recognized Helene's brother and sister-in-law in the crush—a chiropodist who lived in Brooklyn. We chatted for a minute before they went inside.

"Willi here?" I asked.

"Not yet. I didn't see any of them," he said. "Maybe we ought to call up and find out if they're really coming. Between you and me, I never thought the kid would go through with it."

I waited alone just outside the big oaken doors. The air was stifling, and the sun had shifted and faded from behind the clouds darkening the streets. It began to rain. I went into the vestibule, and about three minutes of ten the family arrived.

"A rabbi, I told you," said Willi, folding his dripping umbrella. "He didn't want to take a cab on *Shabbos*. We had to walk here in the rain."

Helene took off her wilted straw hat. "Ruined," she said. The boy said nothing. With a white-silk prayer shawl over his arm, he was dressed in a dark-blue suit that emphasized the pallor of his face. All the color had gone from his cheeks; his lips were drawn and white.

"Congratulations," I told him.

He nodded. "We're late," said his father. "We

ought to get seated." He took his wife by the elbow and they went inside. The boy hung back and pulled at my sleeve.

"D-d-d-do you think they'll l-laugh?" he asked.

"Of course not."

He shook his head and shrugged.

"I p-p-p-prayed and p-p-prayed."

We all sat in the front pew, to the left of the Ark. There were baskets of red roses set on the marble steps. The bronze doors of the Ark were open and the rabbi, young and handsome, wearing horn-rimmed glasses and prematurely gray at the temples, conducted the morning service. He was sweating and, while the cantor sang, he surreptitiously plucked a handkerchief from the sleeve of his robe and dabbed at his upper lip. The service went on, mostly in Hebrew, chanting and responsive reading, the drone of voices and the tinkle of silver bells as Willi and Mr. Goldman were called upon to elevate the Torah over the heads of the congregation and lay it open on the mahogany podium set on the edge of the steps. The rain beat against the stained glass windows. Danny sat to my right, picking at the cuticle of his thumb. When it came time for the recitation of the Haftorah, the Goldman kid went first. He would do well and he knew it—chanting the Hebrew in a high sing-song voice that was just beginning to crack; rather good-looking, and tall for his age, with reddish blond hair, full lips, and pimpled cheeks. His father, seated on the stage to the rabbi's left and next to Willi, beamed at the audience. Then it was Danny's turn. The crowd shifted perceptively in their seats, and as he stood up two women in the row behind us nervously began to fan themselves with their prayer books. Evidently he was right: the Goldman boy had told everyone about his stammer. You could sense it. You could hear everyone in the place take a deep breath as he mounted the three steps with the fringed end of his prayer shawl dragging along the floor. He stood behind the opened Torah, and with a bitten forefinger found his place. The rustle of silks; the audience had shifted again, with a faint murmur. The wooden pews creaked and the noise must have startled him, because he suddenly glanced up. For a moment he was up to his old tricks, trying to stare them down, but it was no use. No one said anything. All at once he was just listening to the sound of their labored breathing. They pitied him and he knew it, and they hated him, in spite of themselves, for the embarrassment that he was causing them, and he was aware of that too. The rabbi wiped the sweat from his upper lip. With his left hand rubbing the side of his nose, Willi sat looking at his feet. Then, for a moment more, wide-eyed, and with trembling lips, the boy continued to stare down at the crowd until he caught my eye. He blinked and shrugged his shoulders again, and hunched forward, as though before he began to stammer the blessing he had made up his mind to assume the burden of what the reiteration of the Law of his Fathers had demanded from the first.

A Pile of Stones

"DEAR MILTON," Nina writes.

"We had a tragedy a day or so after the card I sent you. Bill was drowned. He hadn't swum in the ocean for such a long time, he couldn't resist that treacherous water. The undertow knocked him off his feet, and up against some rocks. I know that you will be greatly saddened by the news.

"I am with his family in Greenwich for a few days. Then I will go back to my parents in New Canaan for the rest of the summer. After that, I'm not sure what I will do. Perhaps come to New York, and get my M.S. at the Columbia University School of Social Work. But I'm still terribly shocked. I just wanted to let you know, for I know that you loved him. . . ."

I can't find the card. It was mailed about a week ago, from Bar Harbor, where they had gone to spend the first two weeks of July. According to Bill's last letter, written to me at the beginning of May, they were going on vacation to celebrate his promotion. He had just been made a full partner in his father's law firm in Stamford, in charge of all the corporate litigation. It was his special interest when I knew him at Yale Law School. And he was good at it. Not brilliant, but hard-working, with something of a reputation on campus for being a grind.

It's one of the ways I remember him best: at two o'clock in the morning, with his stockinged feet up on his desk, and a copy of *Wigmore on Evidence* open in his lap, alternately taking a deep drag from his cigarette and scribbling a note on the pad of lined yellow paper fixed to the steel clipboard he always carried with him to class.

As far as I know, the only outside interest he had was a religious study group he had organized with five or six divinity students and two undergraduates who met twice a month, on Sundays, after morning services at a local Presbyterian church. Church-going for its own sake didn't particularly compel him. Sometimes he went, and sometimes he didn't. He never missed a meeting of the study group, though, and in the week before it met spent most of his spare time reading religious books. He poured through Tillich and Niebuhr, somebody or other by the name of Bonhoeffer, and, just after Thanksgiving, a writer, he said, who ought to interest me very much.

"Who's that?" I wanted to know.

"Martin Buber. We're having a discussion next Sunday on his interpretation of Hassidism. What's the matter? He's a great Jewish thinker. You ought to be very proud."

He showed me the photo of the bearded old man on the cover of the paperback edition of his *Tales of the Hassidim.*

"He looks like my grandfather."

"Then why don't you come on Sunday?" Bill said. "All we do is have brunch and sit around and talk. It's very informal. You might enjoy it."

"I'd like to, really, but I can't. I won't be here. I've got a date in New York on Saturday night."

He never asked me to a meeting again. But Buber and Hassidism! It was all I heard from him. He typed over his favorite Hassidic story and thumbtacked it to the wall over his desk.

"Well, what do you think?" he demanded, when I had read it through twice.

"It's very interesting. Very nicely written. Nice and concise."

"But a lot of crap as far as you're concerned."

"No, I wouldn't go so far as to say that."

"Then what?" he insisted.

"Well, for one thing, you have to believe that prayer works."

"And you don't."

"To tell you the truth, I never think about it. I haven't prayed since I was a kid."

"What happened?"

"I grew up."

He grinned—"touché"—and lit a cigarette, blowing the smoke from his nose, while I read the story once again. I can't remember the exact words. It was the one explaining the biblical injunction against using a metal tool to shape a sacrificial altar. The point being that God more often responds to a rough heaping up of stones; that is to say, a spontaneous, unpremeditated cry from the heart.

"Did you ever study any Hebrew?" he asked me, sitting down on the bed.

"Some. For my Bar Mitzvah, when I was a kid."

"Can you read that?" He pointed to the Yale motto emblazoned on the back of the rocking chair he had bought when he was an undergraduate, and still kept in his room.

"No. Let me see. How do you like that? I don't think I ever noticed it was in Hebrew before."

"It was once a required language here, you know."

"I had no idea."

"Oh yes. And not just for divinity students, either, but for all the undergraduates, along with Latin and Greek. My great-great-grandfather learned his Hebrew at Yale."

"What did he do with it after he graduated?"

"Prayed in it."

"A Presbyterian?"

"You'd be surprised. He came from Vermont, and at that time, in New England, it wasn't that unusual."

"Well, if I could, I'd put in a good word for you myself."

"Yes," he laughed. "It wouldn't do any harm."

And so it went, our whole final year, when we were rooming opposite each other, in Sterling, on the third floor. When Spring vacation came, and I was packing to leave for New York, he wanted to know if my parents were going to celebrate the Passover the following week.

"No. Well, yes, in a way," I said. "We generally have a family get-together, but no religious service, or anything like that. A big dinner."

"And your mother makes gefüllte fish."

"No, Pearl."

"Who's that?"

"The colored maid."

He burst out laughing, and then looked at his watch. "What time does your train leave?"

"Six-fifteen."

"You've got a couple of hours. Why don't you come over to Payne Whitney with me and take a swim. The exercise will do you good."

He was beginning to put on a little weight around his middle, and generally worked out once or twice a week to keep in shape. While I took a quick dip and dried off, he swam his usual twenty laps, and came up the ladder at the deep end of the pool, gasping for breath.

"I want to apologize," he said, jumping up and down on one foot to get the water out of his ears.

"For what?"

"For asking so many questions."

"Forget it."

We got dressed and strolled back to the dorm. "It's hard for me to explain," he went on, as I opened the door to my room. "It's just that ever since I was a kid, He's been very real to me as a Jew. I mean as an actual Jew who once lived. . . . Have you ever read the *Spiritual Exercises of Ignatius Loyola?*"

"No."

"It's not important." He sat down while I finished packing. "When I was ten or twelve, there was only one Jewish family living in town, or one religious Jewish family. An old man who owned a clothing store, who wore a long black beard, and what-do-you-call-them? You know what I mean. The long curls. . . ."

"*Payis.*"

"Yes, that's the word. The curls tucked behind the ears. I can't even remember his name. He and his wife lived in one of the red-brick houses near the railroad station, on Old Steamboat Road. They never had any kids." He paused for a moment, thinking. "Goldfarb! That was his name! 'A Jew, a real live Jew' was all I could think whenever I saw him. Not so much like Him, perhaps, but maybe Joseph. Yes, why not? It was entirely possible that Joseph looked something like that when he was an old man, with that black skull-cap and scraggly beard. And from there, of course, almost without thinking, it was easier to picture the Son when I prayed. Younger, of course, much younger, and maybe taller and thinner, but with the same bushy eyebrows, and the three furrows on His forehead that made a 'V' when he frowned. You know the way kids are. The kind of pictorial imagination they have. And it was much easier for me to pray with some sort of real picture before me. Then too, in a certain way, I was right. What I mean to say is, He was human too. That's the mystery of the thing. . . ."

What puzzled me, of course, was why he hadn't gone to Divinity School to begin with, and become a pro.

"That's exactly why," he explained one afternoon, about a month before graduation, when I had gone into his room to borrow some of his class notes.

"I don't understand."

"A professional!" He grimaced. "How can anyone presume to be able to inspire a bunch of people at, say, ten o'clock sharp every Sunday morning for the rest of your life? And particularly if you're getting paid to do it? Hell, no. That's why Buber's anomism is so significant. I'd rather be an ordinary lawyer who only goes to church when he really feels the need."

"What's anomism?" I asked.

"Well, roughly, that it doesn't make so much difference what you do, but how it's done. In what spirit. When you pray, for instance. . . ." But he caught the expression on my face, and let it go at that. "Never mind. It's getting late. What was it you wanted?"

"Yesterday's class notes on *Bennedict versus Ratner.*"

The rays of the late afternoon sun, vibrating with dust, and turning an orange-red, streamed through the slats in the venetian blinds and struck him in the eyes. He raised his hands in front of his face. "On the clipboard. No, to your left, under the manila folder, on the desk. I've haven't finished typing them up. . . ."

But I'm almost finished with his story. The trouble is that in reading over what I've written so far—and I've tried to get it all down as accurately as I can—nothing he said makes much more sense to me now than it did then. Nor would it to Nina, either, which just doesn't seem fair. They met after graduation, at a party that following October, to be exact, given by Bill's parents to celebrate his passing the Connecticut

Bar Exams. If I remember correctly, her father is a judge. In any case, she was a Sarah Lawrence graduate, a Psych major, who had been brought up as a Congregationalist. The first time that we were introduced, she told me that the only interest she had in religion was in getting Bill to walk down the aisle of a church. He laughed, and gave her a kiss on the mouth. This was after they had been going steady for a couple of months. They came down to New York on a Saturday night, just before Christmas, to go to the theater, and I met them for drinks at the old Sherry-Netherland bar.

"You two ought to get along very well," he said, waving at the waiter for another round.

"I can see it," I told him.

"He's crazy, of course," Nina said to me. "Stark raving mad."

"Of course," I nodded.

"He isn't, though," she added after a pause, with an exaggerated scowl. "That's the problem. He's completely sane. It's very disconcerting. According to the best authorities, a religious maniac ought to have an absolutely rampant Oedipus complex, a desperate need to placate the father. But he doesn't. Not a sign of it. I was absolutely brilliant in abnormal psychology, and I ought to know."

Bill laughed again. The waiter put down three more bourbon and waters. "Of course," she continued,

"I'll grant you that I'm not exactly an objective judge of his condition. As far as I can see . . ." Bill put his hand on her arm.

"Merry Christmas," he said, leaning across the table, and kissing her again. "Merry Christmas, Milt."

"Merry Christmas," I said, raising my glass.

"No. Now there's another thing," said Nina, but the pianist to our right, a fairy with wavy blond hair, began to play "Silent Night" and drowned her out.

The coming June, they were married at the New Canaan Congregational Church. For the next two years, Bill and I kept in touch by mail. I've saved all of his letters. The sprawling handwriting and huge margins on the left side of the page remind me of his class notes.

". . . It's lovely," he wrote, just after his father had bought them a home in Greenwich, on Old Bedford Road. "A converted ice-house, on four and a half acres of land, with a pond and an apple orchard. Nina makes sour applesauce. Milt, I never would have believed it was possible to be so happy. It's a little scary, to tell you the truth. I wonder why? I must ask Nina what Freud would say about that. Right now, she's washing her hair. Tomorrow is Sunday, but I shall sleep late and miss church. No matter. Sometimes I pray here. At night, particularly, when she's asleep. She sleeps on her back, with her hands above her head, the fists clenched.

Last night, I woke up, and looked at her, and thought, 'God above, what more can a man want? Just let it go on and on, and when it comes time for it to end, let me be the first one to go. Take me. . . .' "

Etc., etc., dated August 10, 1961. Eleven months later, he was dead.